Praise for
Big Lonesome

"Joseph Scapellato writes like Wallace Stegner on peyote, Nathanael West in a sweat lodge, Larry McMurtry on a vision quest. *Big Lonesome* whirls the icons of the American West through his virtuosic kaleidoscope. Each story is zany and surreal, yes, but also ferociously real, every page veined with surprise and insight and heartbreak and wonder. Scapellato is an oddball oracle, this book his gobsmackingly original prophecy."

– **CLAIRE VAYE WATKINS**, author of *Gold Fame Citrus*

"In his brilliant, heartbreaking debut story collection, *Big Lonesome,* Joseph Scapellato offers up the only kind of cowboy I hunger for: mythic and flawed and nameless and timeless and horribly, unsettlingly modern. These stories are fantastic."

– **MANUEL GONZALES**, author of *The Regional Office Is Under Attack!*

"The range of virtuosity that Joseph Scapellato displays in *Big Lonesome* is simply astonishing. You want dazzling wordplay? It's here. You want the Old West and the New West, and tales that make myths, break myths, and mock myths? They're here. You want straightforward, realistic fiction in the form of a heartbreaking death-of-love story? Here. A desert race-for-life adventure? Here. So cinch your saddle tight and keep a firm hold on the reins — *Big Lonesome* is a hell of a ride."

– **LARRY WATSON**, author of *Montana 1948*

"If this is what the future sounds like, we have something to celebrate, after all. Joseph Scapellato's *Big Lonesome* is quick and sharp and funny and unlike anything else you've ever read."

– **ROBERT BOSWELL**, author of *Tumbledown, Mystery Ride, Crooked Hearts,* and *The Heyday of the Insensitive Bastards*

"The stories in Joseph Scapellato's *Big Lonesome* are terrifically funny and haunting accounts of people shedding their self-mythologizing ways. On this open range of wrecked memories and dreamscapes, the characters come to terms with their own experiences of pure truth and poisonous truth and humanizing and debasing shame and dirty love and duty love. They learn to live with the many old lonesomenesses dying in them and the new ones trying but failing to kill them. You know that one marvelous tale that has never left you since you first heard it, the one that makes you laugh-cough bloody glass and bright stars every time it comes to your mind? Joseph Scapellato's brilliant *Big Lonesome* offers you twenty-five of them!"

— **KEVIN McILVOY,** author of *Little Peg, Hyssop,* and *The Complete History of New Mexico*

"Joseph Scapellato's *Big Lonesome* is an accomplished debut, a collection of tall tales and campfire stories that create a Wild West unlike any other. With a voice like Barry Hannah channeling Larry McMurtry, Scapellato has updated the cowboy — one of the great American protagonists — into a newly complex, audacious, and utterly contemporary character."

— **MATT BELL,** author of *In the House Upon the Dirt Between the Lake and the Woods*

BIG
LONESOME

stories

Joseph Scapellato

A Mariner Original
Mariner Books

HOUGHTON MIFFLIN HARCOURT

BOSTON • NEW YORK 2017

For information about permission to reproduce selections from this book, write
to trade.permissions@hmhco.com or to Permissions, Houghton Mifflin Harcourt
Publishing Company, 3 Park Avenue, 19th Floor, New York, New York 10016.

www.hmhco.com

Library of Congress Cataloging-in-Publication Data
Names: Scapellato, Joseph, date, author.
Title: Big Lonesome / Joseph Scapellato.
Description: Boston : Mariner Books, 2017.
Identifiers: LCCN 2016029360 (print) | LCCN 2016034756 (ebook) |
ISBN 9780544769809 (paperback) | ISBN 9780544770546 (ebook)
Subjects: LCSH: West (U.S.)—Fiction. | Middle West—Fiction. | BISAC: FICTION /
Short Stories (single author). | FICTION / General. | FICTION / Literary.
Classification: LCC PS3619.C2666 A6 2017 (print) | LCC PS3619.C2666 (ebook) |
DDC 813/.6—dc23
LC record available at https://lccn.loc.gov/2016029360

Book design by Jackie Shepherd

Printed in the United States of America
DOC 10 9 8 7 6 5 4 3 2 1

The following stories first appeared elsewhere, in slightly different form: "Company" in
No Tokens; "Horseman Cowboy" in *North American Review;* "Snake Canyon" in *Third Coast;*
"We Try to Find the Spring in Spring Rock Park in Western Springs, Illinois" in *Hayden's
Ferry Review Online;* "Big Lonesome Endings" (published in sequenced shorts as "The
Train to Pennsylvania," "Pennsylvania," "The Woods," "The Cave," and "The Words") in
Unsaid 7; "Small Boy" in *New Ohio Review;* "One of the Days I Nearly Died" in *Green Moun-
tains Review Online;* "The Veteran" in *PANK 10;* "Western Avenue" in *Curbside Splendor;* "It
Meant There Would Be More" in *LUMINA;* "Fourteen Cowboys by the Fire" in *Necessary
Fiction;* "Drunk in Texas, Two New Friends Talked Horses" in *Pebble Lake Review;* "That-
away" (published as "Brown Boy") in *Puerto del Sol;* "Big Lonesome Middles" (published
in sequenced shorts as "Morning in New Mexico," "Mornings in New Mexico," "Texas
in Texas," and "Afternoon in New Mexico") in *Unsaid 6;* "Immigrants" in > *kill author 16;*
"Driving in the Early Dark, Ted Falls Asleep" in *The Collagist;* "Life Story" in *Kenyon Review
Online;* "Father's Day" in *Post Road;* "Big Lonesome Beginnings" (published in sequenced
shorts as "One Night Near Texas" and "Many Nights Near Texas") in *Unsaid 5;* "Cowboy
Good Stuff's Four True Loves" in *The Collagist;* and "Mutt-Face" (published as "Mutt-Face
Meets Himself") in *Gulf Coast.*

for my family, my friends,
and Dustyn

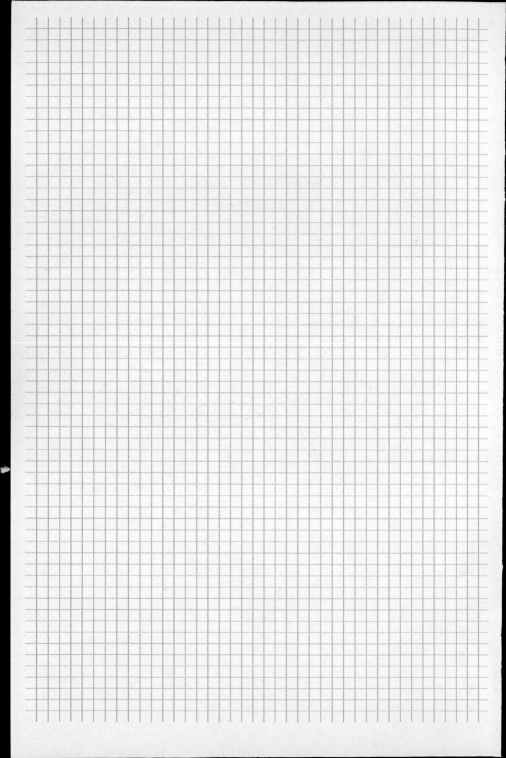

Life is bad. You're lucky when it goes good.
— SCHOOLTEACHER FRANK

Shoot the boot!
— COWGIRL MARGIE

contents

OLD WEST

Big Lonesome
Beginnings

ONE NIGHT NEAR TEXAS

The cowboy sat up and shuddered. Again she wasn't with him, his tent bigger and brighter than that room. In here his body felt unhelpful. He shook his boots from the ground and pulled them on. He stepped out.

His fellow cowboys, their tents, the fire, the herd—all slumping at the bottom of the bowl of night. The way-off mountains wiped out. Burned Down Dan, who never had a tent, just a guitar, slept drunk before the fire, his guitar tucked like a tied-up bedroll between his blistered arms and chin.

The cowboy stared at that guitar, at the fire's hard flicker in its polish, and wondered why he'd woken up. He wondered why he was here instead of with her in that room. The air smelled enough like rain to make him think it might, but the sky wasn't having it.

He stole Burned Down Dan's guitar from Burned Down Dan's arms.

He crouched inside his tent and taught himself to play.

His fingers stumbled. The tent around him sucked smaller.

MANY NIGHTS NEAR TEXAS

He played. Even when he didn't, he did. His playing wasn't only in his head. His playing was all over.

When he played outside himself, with fingers and strings and frets, he made it sound like there were four guitars showing up inside the one, and all four were loners, loners yoked into a team, a team that listened to itself and got on well with other folks and animals and any kind of nighttime sky.

His fellow cowboys stayed awake to listen on account of how sleeping meant missing out on what his music had them feeling. They never said much, just sat there on their bedrolls trying not to look too lonesome, their faces crossed with firelight, their jaws working jerky and tobacco and fingernails and knives. Who knew what was worked in their hearts.

Something, because the cowboy's playing never failed to magnetize: men and women alike would bend, favoring his direction, and when he stopped, they wouldn't be sneaky about it, they'd sidle right over and find reasons to touch his body — slaps on the back and slugs to the arm, handshakes, hugs, kisses. Always friendly.

What he found curious about all of this was this: when they touched him after an evening of playing, he couldn't feel their bodies. It was like his skin was double-thick, deadened, and asleep. He couldn't feel anything except an aching to be feeling his music touching him.

He knew his music would never be a body but he played it nonetheless.

Horseman Cowboy

Called, horseman cowboy clops over to old man foreman like he isn't.

Old man foreman, the range boss, dying for days on a dirty blanket, he squints way up at horseman cowboy, saying, "Horseman cowboy, don't none of us know just how you came to be, where or what you from. All we know is what you know. All man, all horse. Oats and beef, hay and steaks, mares and whores. The range, the range, the range, but always bumping plumb into a border."

Horseman cowboy, ten feet tall from hoof to head, big chin set and big arms crossed, he looks way out westward over blistered land, saying, "Sure is so."

"Top cutter, pegger, roper," says old man foreman, "no saddle and no spurs and no bridle needed, clear-footed, with bottom. Every day we say it: you your own mount."

The other ranch hands, hats off, young and sun-crusted, flanking old man foreman, they nod like they're at church and sorry.

Old man foreman rolly-eyes how he rolly-eyes when he's talking scripture.

"Your face, your chest, your arms," he shouts, "they nailed to the center of a compass the points of which are white man, black man, brown man, red man! Your withers, your back, your croup, they nailed to the center of a compass the points of which are saddlebred, quarter, appaloosa, mustang!"

One by one the ranch hands drop their eyes to their boots in shamed awe.

Horseman cowboy, iron-shoed and woolen-shirted, bearded, the skin of his man-body sunned, the coat of his horse-body coarse, he looks way out eastward over scabby land, saying, "So?"

"The men," says old man foreman, wringing the dirtiest ends of the dirty blanket, "my men, me, us, we look to you and can't be other than sure you're so. To see you with so much already, and so done with it? It makes a man feel small and foul inside. It makes a man grip to things he ain't so sure he believes, to believe in the gripping, the gripping-to."

Horseman cowboy says, "I'm a-going."

"What all's wrong with you is you can't see what all's right with you," says old man foreman.

Horseman cowboy drill-pisses into the dry grass.

The ranch hands watch the golden frothing in a state of holy wonder.

Old man foreman flings a canteen, screaming, "Catch some up, boys, and quick—it just might save my dying life!"

Horseman cowboy rears and goes.

Horseman cowboy fucks a horse, a donkey, a mule—he kick-smashes trees and boulders and hills—he bellows black rage to a moonless star-pricked sky—

Educated circus man, fat and wily, cane-waving, strolling through the stinking air of his biggest big-top tent, he says to horseman cowboy in a brightly painted voice, "Homo Equinus Gladitorius! The Four-Footed Bridge Between Barbarism and Civilization, Between Bestial Animal Appetite and Elevated Human Refinement! Behold: the Celebrated Incelibate Centaur!"

Horseman cowboy stands still, his big face blank.

Educated circus man presents to horseman cowboy a copper-painted tin helmet, a copper-painted tin breastplate, and a copper-painted tin spear. He smiles a smile that says more than the crooked mouth that makes it.

The other circus acts—acrobats and animal tamers, sword swallowers and fire-eaters, dwarves and giants, freaks of a physical, foreign, and manufactured nature—they to-and-fro with costumes and props and makeup, acting as if they aren't studying horseman cowboy.

Horseman cowboy crushes the copper-painted tin helmet and shreds the copper-painted tin breastplate and hurls the copper-painted tin spear through the way-up billowing big-top tent roof. He says, "My hat."

With his cane, educated circus man hands horseman cowboy his cowboy hat.

Horseman cowboy eats his cowboy hat.

The circus acts stop to-and-froing. They suppress grins and cheers.

Horseman cowboy horseshits on the packed dirt.

Educated circus man cane-pokes the horseshit into a pickling jar. "Will our Celebrated Incelibate Centaur Master One of the Two Worlds He Canters Into? or, Impossibly, Both? or, Tragicomically, Neither?"

Horseman cowboy rears and goes.

Horseman cowboy fucks a wolf, a cougar, a bear—he kick-smashes shacks and sheds and fences—he bellows black sorrow to a sky slashed by a bladed moon—

Refined reformer woman, principled and accomplished, scalpel-faced, sitting in the sitting room of her sober mansion, she says to horseman cowboy in a letter-to-the-editor voice, "Taught, you shall teach the multitude of needy others. Your instruction shall be deep in understanding, owing to your innate and, in this instance, invaluable familiarity with the lay of the swamp of savagery. You shall stand outside this savagery and speak to those who sludge about inside it, nose-deep in ignorance: Indians, immigrants, criminals, lunatics, degenerates, perverts, Catholics. With you present in our Homes and Institutions, with the Lord in you, using you as He has used chosen others, we might together and in humility hasten the Coming of the Kingdom of God to this nation."

Horseman cowboy, horse-sitting, drinks his hot tea in one gulp.

The other reformer women, also refined, sit in a pious circle of chairs. They nod at their leader's speech, but inwardly repeat silent prayers to protect themselves from the feelings that shudder through their bodies as they smell horseman cowboy's manly horse-musk, his horsey man-musk.

Refined reformer woman tilts her teacup. It's empty. "All are incomplete before the Lord," she says. "This path will lead you into completion."

Horseman cowboy stands. His horse-sized man-dick waggles.

Refined reformer woman sighs a sigh that isn't saying if it's made of mostly pity or disgust. "It is plain to see that what you would appear to be when in the public eye differs, woefully, from what you are when you are alone, shackled simply to yourself."

Horseman cowboy stares at her. His stare is long and shallow.

"Or is the matter much worse, and worsening?" says refined reformer woman, curious but unconcerned.

Horseman cowboy bobs his head politely, saying, "Ma'am."

One by one the other reformer women pale, praying for horseman cowboy to go and stay at once, to be nearby but distant, to return only to depart only to return only to depart, forever.

Horseman cowboy rears and goes.

Horseman cowboy fucks a woman, a woman, a woman—he kick-smashes haystacks and wells and barns—he bellows black longing to a sky swollen with a half-moon's glowing ache—

Willful farm girl, strong and season-wise, wide-handed, milking a spooked cow in the dark warmth of the barn, she says to horseman cowboy in a master-to-apprentice voice, "I done told you. We stake our acres way out, in the Territory. Away from Ma and Pa, my brothers and sisters and uncles and cousins. We raise up our home. We start our family."

The other spooked cows shuffle in their stalls, lowing.

Horseman cowboy stands at the barn door. His stare is short and deep. The barn door is creaking closed behind him.

Willful farm girl says, "I seen both sides of you, how each throws mud on the other. It's a devil's trick. When you make that you can't be but one way, it ain't even near right, it's just it's what you're choosing."

Horseman cowboy turns himself around.

Willful farm girl slams the milk bucket. "I done killed chickens and roosters and cows and horses and buried little brothers and big sisters and should it come to it I will bury the baby you're leaving me with. I will not weep until you go."

Horseman cowboy goes.

Horseman cowboy fucks a pile of pitchforks, hoes, and scythes —he kick-smashes railroad ties and switching stations and bridge pillars—he bellows black loathing to a sky sick with the shine of a nearly full moon—

Young railroad baron, handsome, clean, smelling of shoeshine and fruit, touring his company's track as its lengths are laid by his company's laborers, he says to horseman cowboy in a voice tucked between shares of stock and bills of sale, "All are yoked to labor. You, like me, are made to labor more mightily than others. Find with me the task that suits your size. Labor mightily for me, for Progress, so that lesser others might ride upon what we lay to greatness."

The laborers, men of as many colors as tongues, hammer and haul and grunt. They see but don't acknowledge horseman cowboy. They labor. They lose fingers, hands, and limbs.

Young railroad baron offers horseman cowboy a bottle of sherry.

Horseman cowboy drinks it all and eats the bottle. He says, "Ain't nothing can make them who ain't great great."

Young railroad baron claps horseman cowboy on the horse-haunches and laughs the laugh that is slipped between bribes. "We are alike; we see that what we say and what we believe must be different—different but partnered, harnessed. All you lack is the proper yoke. Allow me to yoke you."

Horseman cowboy eats young railroad baron.

The laborers labor.

Horseman cowboy fucks a nest of snakes, a family of alligators, a beached riverboat—he kick-smashes boardwalks and docks and wharves—he bellows black hatred to a sky saddled with a full moon's wide and crushing weight—

One-eyed one-eared whaling captain, crunchy-faced, incredulous, standing on the deck of a great ship, looks down at the dock at horseman cowboy and shouts in a shouting-through-sea-swells voice, "A steed a Mate on a ship! On a ship, a steed a Mate—why, who has heard of it, seen of it, met with it? Me, I have heard and seen and met with many a thing I never once thought to in the hold and on deck, by the flicker of the binnacle, in the watery wasteland's blinding noontime light, on eerie shores shaped by agents neither natural nor unnatural—but aye, call me Sicilian if it be so, never once a steed a Mate on a ship."

The other mates, on board, in drink and song and smoke, they cackle and curse with relish.

Horseman cowboy's stare is up-front and orders-ready.

One-eyed one-eared whaling captain knock-knocks the railing. "Blast my blood! Have you lately bathed in the harbor, or is that a bilge-load of sweat I see upon your face and shoulders?"

A plank cracks beneath one of horseman cowboy's hooves. He shifts, clopping.

One-eyed one-eared whaling captain says, "Do you swim, now?"

Horseman cowboy says, "If it ain't deep."

Horseman cowboy fucks a road, an avenue, a boulevard—he kick-smashes cobblestones and hitching posts and gas lamps—he bellows black fear to a sky made panicked by the waning moon—

Weary foreign mesmerist, consumptive and tubercular, bloated, stuffed into the lone chair at the lone table in his smoky salon, he says to horseman cowboy in a voice burdened by decades of belief, "In you, in me, in all: Vital Magnetic Fluid. What is for health? What is for ill? What is for to go from one to the other? Vital Magnetic Fluid. Vital Magnetic Fluid. Vital Magnetic Fluid."

Horseman cowboy, horse-sitting, blinks at the wall. His stare is limp and thin.

The other visitors, educated, refined, willful, young, one-eyed or one-eared, they sit in chairs at the back of the salon and wait their turn. They only see themselves: the selves they are and were, the selves they might be, and the selves set like posts between these selves.

Weary foreign mesmerist says, "My Vital Magnetic Fluid,

most-concentrated, is to order your Vital Magnetic Fluid, most-dispersed. But you must look."

Weary foreign mesmerist says, "You must look to me."

Weary foreign mesmerist says, "Look."

Trembling, horseman cowboy looks.

Horseman cowboy fucks no one, nobody, nothing. He doesn't kick-smash anything. He doesn't bellow any black feeling to any sort of sky.

For he doesn't know how many days he doesn't know where he is.

In this state, he for the first time feels age sink into his body. Age treats his man- and horse-parts just the same, clutching to what it can in an attempt to slow itself. That it's small surprises him. That this surprise delights him saddens him. When he knows where he is again, he is wanting.

Wanting what?

Horseman cowboy fords a river half-dammed with a rotten roof.

Resentful transcendentalist poet, regionally famous, well-dressed but dirty, swinging on his country-cottage porch swing, he says in a reading-out-loud voice to horseman cowboy, "Trust your impulses. Track them, in trust, to your inner temple. Enter in awe. Worship at the altar of yourself, acknowledging that the altar, the worship, the entrance, the tracking, and the impulse will differ when you meet them next. Find this, all of this, now. Find this again."

The porch swing mumbles. Birds squirt strange calls. The light through the trees is yellow-green. A blistered leaf, scabby with insect eggs, flits onto horseman cowboy's bare chest.

Horseman cowboy says, "Done all that already."

Resentful transcendentalist poet lights a pipe, clouding the face he's making. Through the cloud he says, "Make art."

Horseman cowboy fucks art until art fucks him back, and he kick-smashes art until art kick-smashes him flat, and he bellows black feelings into art until art, heavy and full and whole, bellows empty again.

The moon gives off a damaged glow behind a cloud the size of the sky.

Horseman cowboy grows older.

Horseman cowboy quits for good on fucking, kick-smashing, and bellowing. He lives between a city and a countryside, and then a ranch and a range, and then a long road and a jagged arroyo. He moves more slowly. Feels more slowly. Thinks.

Wants?

Horseman cowboy dreams back the places and the folks he could have stuck to. He dreams back the nights he bellowed, kick-smashed, and fucked under. He tries to make a trail from the places and the folks to the nights, but can't. The tracks are covered.

Horseman cowboy feels sick.

So?

Horseman cowboy is old. His skin wrinkles, his coat dulls. His hands and hooves ache and crack. From the places he lives, he watches dust and fog and star-paths, cattle and cowboys, injured outlaws, families of displaced tribes and settlers, wild starving horses. He watches without rage or sorrow, no longing and no loathing, no hatred, no fear.

Horseman cowboy is very old. He wears as many blankets as he has. He's sick.

So?

Horseman cowboy can't see what's saying "so."

Whatever it is, whatever it wants, it's keeping at it.

So?

Horseman cowboy chews his blankets.

Whatever it is, whatever it wants, it's going away.

It goes away.

Under his blankets, horseman cowboy follows whatever goes away into himself. He finds a border behind a border, and in both, more borders. They are all too far to cross.

Thataway

The hard-luck cowboy hauled his garbage bag into the laundromat. He'd walked the whole way from the edge-of-town motel. The sky was bright but the day was brown, the sun buried, a windstorm threshing desert dirt into fields of glowing haze. The walk had taken the hard-luck cowboy an hour and then some on busted sidewalks and shoulders. He'd passed barren strip malls and trash-pierced tumbleweeds. The air teemed with debris. His boots chewed his bare feet. Blown grit pocked his face and caked his body.

Earlier, when he'd coughed himself awake, sniffed his shirts, pulled the room's garbage bag inside out to stuff it with his clothes, and stepped into the parking lot, he'd discovered he didn't know what the hell had happened to his pickup.

When he wasn't in motels he was living in his pickup. When he wasn't in his pickup he was working. When he wasn't working he was spending weeks high on whatever could be had, crooking himself into something slow and wooden, something proofed against surprise. Not dumb, but damn near it. Despite the onset of this condition his face had a shape plenty of gals found fine. They were drawn to how the good looks had just begun to splinter. The ones with big hearts would think, Care and oil can help this keep.

The laundromat popped in stale light: a chunky couple texting, a boyish-looking caped girl gnawing on an action figure, a manager pushing a push broom. One long bench per wall. In the corner, a tattooed pregnant gal folded bedsheets, speaking Spanish to someone hidden by a paint-crackled pillar. The layered odors each uncurled: flowers, fruit, ammonia, rot.

The hard-luck cowboy was a man of many habits—this was his line for gals when they asked him how he made his living—with one of his habits being to shake out his clothes before shoving them into the washing machine. He whip-cracked his jeans. Baby roaches scattered, little brown-black buttons. They zipped off to the darkness beneath a nearby garbage bin.

In this manner he readied and loaded the clothes he owned, one at a time, each article pregnant with odors, the odors pregnant with images, images the hard-luck cowboy recognized but couldn't feel one way or the other about—a beer-soaked blanket in the bed of his pickup; a dumpy backroom at Dixon's; three tidy children on one gal's couch; a kiss—and when he shut the lid, an old man was standing by his side.

Standing mighty close.

Unfazed, the cowboy dug for quarters.

The mighty close old man said, "Son, that your pickup out there?"

The cowboy didn't look.

"Brown," said the mighty close old man. "Color of dirt, what we come from."

The cowboy rang coins into the slot. He had himself a sideways gander through the shaded window at his brown pickup. Both headlights smashed.

A windbreaker flapped onto the hood ornament, then off and away.

"I knowed a brown boy once," said the mighty close old man.

The cowboy came up two quarters short. The mighty close old man snapped down a stack of coins and said, "I can't figure what he was other'n brown. Skin brown. Hair brown. Eyes, even where they was black, was brown brown brown."

Borrowed quarters in, the cowboy cranked the machine to cold wash and squared off with the mighty close old man, whose clumped-together face was as unrecognizable as roadkill, profoundly unfamiliar, unlike the face of anyone the cowboy had ever met and forgotten. Only the tongue was alive, wild with pinkness.

"Brown as what," said the cowboy, not friendly.

The mighty close old man looked at the cowboy like the cowboy had asked him where the sky was. Last night this had been the cowboy's habit—asking anyone who walked into Dixon's, Where's the sky?

Swinging pool cues, Where's the sky?

Punting barstools, Where's the sky?

Humping strangers, Where's the sky?

A bag of drugs, a dying dog, a terrified kid who calls him Dad; the cowboy howling, Sky, where the fuck you been? Sky, what the fuck you think you are anyhow?

"Brown brown brown," answered the mighty close old man.

Filthy wind heaved against the laundromat's window-walls and the hard-luck cowboy was reminded of the grime worked into his skin and mouth, into his sleeveless t-shirt and jeans, between his forehead and bandana. He flicked flaky dirt-boogers out of an armpit. When his clothes were clean and dry, he promised himself, he'd change right into them, right here. Then he'd linger in the laundromat for as long as he damn well liked, patting himself, feeling how little time one got with clean clothes, how the act of donning them u-turned them back to dirty dead ends.

Most things are like that, he thought.

"I seen that brown boy *there*," said the mighty close old man, angling his chin at the bench behind them. On its slats crawled the caped girl who looked like a boy. She'd removed the action figure from her mouth, a caped monkey, and was jamming its head into bench-ruts.

The cowboy spat a dark glob into the garbage bin. It plocked. The way the old man was carrying on—a cut-rate compound of pride, impotence, and desperation—reminded the cowboy of how he himself would get when he'd get riled, when all he wanted was to father that rile in any son of a bitch in range. He didn't like it, recognizing himself like that.

With disrespect, the cowboy said, "I bet."

The mighty close old man shuffled so near the cowboy that he seemed about to kiss him. "You tell me," said the mighty close old man. "You tell me what you think brown boy saw when brown boy looked me in the eye."

The most regular habit the hard-luck cowboy had was not sharing much about himself with others. He didn't share much about himself with himself either. When he thought about this, which wasn't often, and only ever right before he'd stride into that part of the afternoon or evening he knew he'd only half-remember, he always acknowledged that even to himself he was a somebody else, an image he'd made, spitting or not, that he didn't feel one way or the other about. He turned to walk past the mighty close old man.

But the old fellow backstepped and thrust his hand so that the cowboy walked plumb into his palm. Then he raised his other hand and slapped it to himself. His face twitched; different parts began to tremble at different speeds. He whooped, "A showdown!—brown boy's eyeing me and I'm eyeing back, we're mean, meaner than a pair of razor-bladed roosters set a-loose in the same coop, staring on and on by that there bench and next thing I know, *whang!* two planks pressed my body, one in front and one behind, they clapped in so heavy my breath bucked out and my arms went dead and jangly, and I can see you ain't had the pleasure but believe me when you do you're in a coffin and it's caving in. What brown boy saw when brown boy stared me down ain't nobody seen before, and when I seen him seeing something where for longer than you've lived I been seeing nothing, well, that made me more than I was, meaning, too much. I opened my mouth—to say who knows what, who's got words for a heart attack 'cause that's what it was, sure as shooting, and something more to boot—and that's when brown boy jumped into my mouth."

The mighty close old man pointed down his gullet with two crooked fingers. His tongue squelched. "Thataway," he said, wiping his hand on his overalls, "brown boy in and climbing cautious like coming down a ladder with two buckets of paint and a baby, which I done once. And you know where he got, and you know what he did?"

"Nope."

The mighty close old man poked the cowboy's chest. "Where he got was my stalling heart. What he did was hug it, tight as a mother hugs her dying child."

"Which I seen once," whispered the mighty close old man.

The cowboy shrugged one shoulder, then the other.

"I survived!"

"You don't look it," said the cowboy.

The mighty close old man gasped in such a way that he offered the cowboy a clear view of his enthusiastic tongue, the most loathsome sight the cowboy could at that moment remember seeing.

"You get it," said the mighty close old man, astounded.

This reaction, so sincere, was not the reaction the cowboy had counted on. It began to rile him. He was well-acquainted with this rile: it had come into him last night after beer and beef jerky and whiskey and blow and muscle relaxants, just as it had come into him many nights before, during bar games or wager-making or the sweet-talking of soused gals. When the rile punched and kicked at the door, the cowboy often let it in, though he took his time in doing so because it might turn away on its own. If he wasn't careful it'd come back a few beers later as the weepies.

The weepies were worse than anything.

Falling down and yowling and fist-waving, blubbering on roofs and under cars and over toilets, into mornings that stumbled up from far away. Wanting to get somewhere. No direction a direction that would work.

Right now the rile was on the porch and peeking in.

Because of this the cowboy turned to walk off without comment, but the old man hopped on the cowboy's boots. Perched, he said, "My question is, what-all will you do with how you get it?"

The cowboy began to say that he'd put it on a cattle prod and twist it up the old man's shit-chute, but before he could finish, the old man gripped the cowboy's throat with both hands and started squeezing. The squeezing didn't hurt. The old man's face went white and quivery—he was choking the cowboy as hard as he could. Standing still, the cowboy flexed his neck. His throat thickened some, like when the weepies came, and the thickening was enough to make him briefly feel something for the old man, a warm and soggy lowness. They shared a susceptibility.

The old man, sweating, spluttered foamy saliva. His hands worked that neck like it was the stuck lid on something good. The cowboy spluttered too, through his nose, blasting sprays of gritty snot.

All the idling others in the laundromat stopped to watch the two men spattering each other, the cowboy looking wooden, the old man looking like he wasn't choking anybody but himself, until the old man grunted and let go his grip and went down like his legs had been illusions. The cowboy, coughing some, stepped over the wheezing old man and walked to the bench where he sat next to the caped girl, who stared at his wooden face in bewildered admiration. She tried to hide how excited she was that he had sat next to her, but couldn't. Her parents returned to texting. They smelled like they'd taken baths in bongwater.

The tattooed pregnant gal and the manager rushed to help the old man up, speaking Spanish to each other and taking turns dealing disgusted glances to the cowboy. They looked exactly like someone the cowboy sort of knew, or at least one of them did, almost, but he couldn't remember who that someone was or what that someone had meant. Maybe he'd been here before, shaking out his clothes, ignoring lonely men, but maybe not. He leaned his head against the window. The glass wobbled, raked by sheets of grit. Being riled was a feeling the cowboy would rather not be feeling. Being riled was a feeling so big, so rowdy, it made you want to grab it hard and crush it — which you couldn't, because it was a feeling. A feeling was a nothing. If you were slow and wooden, feeling wouldn't surprise you, and if feeling didn't surprise you, you could stick to a principle. His principle had mostly been to blame the sky.

What was the sky if not a sack of nothing too?

He peeled off his bandana and scrubbed his face with it. It scratched him pleasurably. Dirt counted as a something, sure, but it came as close to a nothing as a something could. A mostly nothing. Fuck the sky. He opened his eyes. The old man was right there sitting next to him, breathing in wet rasps. The double-loader dinged. The cowboy got up and the old man got up too. His shapeless face flew three colors now: white, yellow, and purple. He followed the cowboy as he transferred his clothes to the dryer. Like before, the cowboy shook each article out. This time no memories arose. He was too riled.

The cowboy returned to the bench. He sat between the parents, who were very stoned, and the caped girl, who was squirming with hesitation. She wanted to touch him. He clenched his teeth, grinding granules of dirt. The old man bent before the caped girl and sweetly requested that she move down, which she was reluctant to do, but did. Beaming, the old man shook her hand, called her a well-raised boy, and gave her a stack of quarters. She frowned at this reward. He took her place. He leaned toward the cowboy until their shoulders touched. He whispered, "Stayed inside me for nine years and a day, all them years they was the best years of my life and I but half-reckoned it and when you but half-reckon it you don't reckon there's another half, which feels honkatonk until the day that other half turns you into chickenfeed because the day brown boy left was like most days, excepting that my son died of drugs my daughter died of being overseas my horse died of getting bit by baby rattlers and my ranch burnt down with my wife on the roof."

The caped girl, listening, dropped her action figure. Her face twisted with tears.

The cowboy, not listening, had been regarding his boots, slashed-up and discolored from forgotten escapes. That they had a better memory of the cowboy's last six months than the cowboy somehow seemed the old man's fault.

With a sad whistle-sigh, the old man patted the cowboy's bare shoulder. He turned the pat into a squeeze and met the angry stare it evoked with the greatest of sympathy and warmth, as if the cowboy had been the one who'd lost everything in one day.

The dryer buzzed. They both stood up but the hard-luck cowboy punched the old man back to the bench, a right hook to the sternum. The old man gulped for air and raised his hand. The cowboy pushed him so that he knocked noggins with the caped girl and they both fell to the floor. One of them began to wail. The cowboy strutted to the dryer but his garbage bag was gone, someone had thrown it away, so he went to the bin and pulled the plastic bag and turned it inside out — pop cans, candy wrappers, bleach, a bloody shirt, brown boy.

The cowboy walked back to the dryer and opened it and started stuffing his hot clothes into the bag.

Brown boy leaped onto the lid, slamming it shut and nearly catching the cowboy by the wrist. He was made of sticks and sludge and his mouth was an oily pulsing hole.

The old man, sneaking up from behind, slapped his hands over the cowboy's mouth and screamed, "WHO YOU COME TO KEEP ALIVE TODAY, BROWN BOY?"

Brown boy oozed, leaking from himself in viscous strands. He was the size of a turkey buzzard and he stank like a vinegaroon. His hands plopped together in prayer.

The manager stepped in front of the tattooed pregnant gal and raised her push broom defensively, and the caped girl's parents restrained her as she struggled to join the cowboy, and the old man tried to pull the cowboy away by the head, but the cowboy, stronger, wanting his clothes, they were his, they were clean, grasped the lid's handle with his free hand and tried to force it open.

"WHO YOU COME TO RUN OUT ON NOW, BROWN BOY?"

Brown boy's eyes were mouths that drooled.

The old man yanked at the cowboy's head as if it were a jammed clutch.

Brown boy stomped the cowboy's hand. The cowboy gasped —his mouth opened, he tasted the old man's linty fingers—his eyes stung—he let the old man wrench him back, his hand sucking out of brown boy's foot with a burp—brown boy staggered forward, melting, shrinking like some foul snowman—together they bumbled to the glass door where they pushed against the weight of the wind and tripped outside into ripping walls of dust. The old man led the way to the brown pickup, threw open the passenger door for the cowboy, then hobbled around to the driver's side. The doors shut, dampening the howls.

The cab was dark, much darker than the sky. Through the windshield and the storm and the shaded window of the laundromat, they couldn't see anyone. The old man banged the doors locked.

"You don't get it," he said, let down.

The muck on the cowboy's hand crusted. He pulled off his sleeveless t-shirt with his clean hand, wiped, wadded the shirt, and ditched it through the back window and into the bed. His hand remained a hideous brown. The stain smelled of something he knew — a carpet? — a wet sandbox? — a brother? — and was not unpleasant, though he sensed it would be for others. He took big whiffs.

"I wouldn't do that," said the old man, locking the back window.

Boiled vegetables, linoleum, a sister?

He hunched, sniffing. He was dizzy with near-knowing.

A future, a present, a past?

The old man jerked the cowboy's hand away from his face and tried to get the cowboy to sit on it. The cowboy drew it back into a fist and told the old man to get the shit-hell out of his goddamned pickup.

"What you're sitting in is mine," said the old man.

The cowboy reexamined the interior. This pickup, neat and stale, in no way resembled his pickup. His pickup wasn't even brown. The rile, which had been so big, important, and lawful, left his body. He returned to sniffing his hand. He needed to smell himself. He needed the smell of himself to spin him into crying. Not into the weepies: straight crying, like a kid.

"Mine," said the old man. He gave the wheel a hesitant touch.

Brown boy appeared at the end of the hood. He was half the size he'd been. The wind wobbled him.

The old man made a show of searching every pocket but couldn't come up with the key. Only a pack of rolling papers tucked behind a visor, and crayons and coloring books stuffed into the glovebox.

Brown boy tried the driver's-side door and then the passenger's. The handles rattled patiently.

The smells in the stain ran out. The cowboy slapped at his hand and smelled again. Nothing. He let it fall into his lap.

"I thought you got it," said the old man. "Then was sure you didn't. Now I just don't know." His face bulged darkly, uniting its patchiness. He sat up more straight. He was having and ignoring a heart attack.

The cowboy felt a skin-rippling chill, and then a head-heat, and then a broad and bodiless itch. Where the rile had been in him now loomed a nothing more nothing than a feeling. Most nothings showed up where a something used to be, and the gone something was what you used to measure the nothing. This nothing had come from where there had never been anything. There was no telling how much of him it would require, and for how long, and to what end. It was much worse than the weepies.

From the bed, brown boy tried the back window.

"I don't get it," said the cowboy, afraid.

The old man reached out to touch the cowboy's shoulder but he couldn't work it right and his arm thumped into the cowboy's lap. He flopped around for the cowboy's hand. Taking it, he said, "Let's the both of us stay here until you do."

The windstorm's dense center closed in. The pickup rocked and creaked.

In the cowboy the nothing expanded inwardly.

Brown boy climbed over the end of the hood. He walked it to the windshield, leaning into the winds that dismantled him, that flayed him of layers. His eyes were whispering.

The old man tugged at the cowboy's hand. He raised his voice, as if talking into a bad ear: "What I need is to relieve you from the notion that you can save yourself."

The cowboy sensed he'd have to do a something.

"Stay with me, now," said the old man.

The cowboy opened the door and slammed it on the old man's scream. The wind raked his bare chest and back, roaring, a whipping and a whirling and a thickening of air, the way-up sun shut out. Brown boy, the size of a crabapple, faced the cowboy. His puny arms opened for a hug. The cowboy grabbed him—he crushed him in his fist, feeling a sharp pop—he opened and cradled his hand. Powdery grains swirled in his palms, no sparkle, no shine. He snorted them.

The old man opened the door and fell out. He closed it from the ground. He stopped moving.

A car horn sounded, either light and close or loud and far.

The cowboy waited for an effect. The wind encrusted him in dirt.

Carrying their bags and baskets, the stoned parents hustled out of the laundromat, jerking along the caped girl, who protested, who visored her eyes with a hand and searched the haze. She was forced into the brown pickup. They didn't see the old man, who they almost stepped on, and they didn't see the cowboy, who they almost flattened as they drove away.

The first stage was a rush of terrible shame. The cowboy's limbs felt full of wet garbage. Next it would get hard to move. He had to move.

He walked across the parking lot and into the highway, toward the center of the heart of the storm. He waved his hands in front of his face, and when he couldn't see them through the mad screen of wind and earth, he stopped. I'm gone, he thought. But he wasn't. And he knew it.

Cowboy Good Stuff's Four True Loves

"HIS FIRST"

A whore. She played her clothes like cards. Even with an empty hand she'd be beaming, singing brassy songs to keep the game going. Her room was small and dark and hot, a miracle she made homey.

When their first time ended she strutted fingers up his arm. She crossed to his chest, kicked a rib, clapped her palm flat. She leaned in close. She whispered that a man could make an unknowing whore of any woman, even ladies, just by what was in his heart when he was with her.

In his heart: her brassy singing.

He listened for a spell. Then said, "Don't you mean what *wasn't?*" She scooted back and up and let her voice break big, singing out in that little room.

He shattered into shivers — goosepimples popping off down every limb — heart stumbling.

Every song she sang she'd call "Good Stuff." The only thing she'd ever say about herself was she used to sing on riverboats in Illinois.

"The ones that come as big as they come."

When he left Oklahoma with the herd he was feeling that kind of big, like he'd see her everywhere. Why not? It was the way he had of making her go unmissing.

When he saw himself in streams and shiny blades, he'd get to humming.

"THE SHORTHORN"

Broke down to her belly by a rocky patch. She'd eaten something foul.

Old Jim Bucket with the split chin saw her first, shouted out, and all the punchers pushed the herd the hell away from there, dust churning up in banks, cowdogs barking, the sun hanging high.

Because the others had the moving covered, Good Stuff rode over to the sickened shorthorn to see what could be done. He passed Old Jim Bucket going thataway, looking gray and pouch-faced, puppet-like, riding hard to fetch the rifle from Flaco. Most said Bucket had been in beef cattle for sixty-five years. When you worked with him, you saw his gift soon enough: the old man had long talks with the animals in his charge, even those that weren't, his words rolling out in English but with different meanings and deliveries—strange tones and speeds, fits and starts. Every sentence a foreigner in familiar clothes, always learning, always feeling out how best to say what needed to be said.

If you watched this your skin prickled. Even so, Bucket was big with high-rolling ranch bosses. He nearly always brought every animal back.

Good Stuff stuck close to Bucket in his early weeks on the job, sneaking in a listen when he could. He saw the old timer strike it up with steers, bulls, heifers, freemartins, muleys, calves, horses, donkeys, dogs, lizards, and beetles, each creature addressed in a special way. Before they left camp, Bucket had been crouching by his tent, pleading to a tarantula. Asking whispered questions while the hairy critter crawled into the shadows of his pant leg.

"Why no you ain't," Bucket said. "You ain't, why no, you, you ain't?"

Good Stuff, pretending to tie his bedroll, whispered Bucket's words to feel how they sat in his mouth.

Bucket, who had now gone to fetch the rifle.

Good Stuff approached the broke-down shorthorn. He dismounted his nervous horse and crunched over slow. The shorthorn's left side was touching rock-shade, her body heaving, her breathing ugly. He reached to caress her. She snuffled her big head away, then back, eyes swimming, legs crushed beneath her bulk.

He sat next to her on a pile of rocks. Dissipated herd-dirt clouded by, five hundred clomping hooves not so noisy now. She bumped him gently with her head.

He opened his mouth to say something and singing came out.

Not words he knew. All made-up.

The words coming from some hard core of feeling he hadn't felt but once before, centered, tight as a knot of clutched-together hands.

Something big at the heart of all those hands.

Unknotting out, and opening—everything he didn't think he had was there—even the melody—until he'd used the words right up. He closed his mouth.

He came back to where he was.

His tongue caked dry. Gleaming black flies. The shorthorn dead.

He turned: the cowboys bent-up on their horses not four paces away, in a half-circle, their moustaches wet. Old Jim Bucket looking like he'd been shot in the throat. The sun squeezing low, swabbing all their faces bright.

"HIS SECOND"

Sheriff's daughter, a schoolteacher. Smart and stout and something else with her hands on her hips.

He gave up cowboying to stay with her near Amarillo, his idea being to learn carpentry. When they went for walks along the town's parched creek they got to feeling there were parts of each other they didn't know they had, but had always had, and here they were learning to use those parts to grab on and let go and hold tight. He kicked sticks out of her way and steered them clear of snakes. She blushed, told him what she'd been teaching. He made up songs, his singing coming out in real words, words they knew, and she stopped to sit on stones and write the verses down. When they held hands, roads rose up, bending from behind some way-off mountain. They were the kind of roads you cleared yourself. The kind that came with ranches and children and dogs, well-digging, feed-storing, song-playing on the porch you built on the land you owned, a song for every day, every day a road, every road crooking back to its beginning.

Sometimes they held hands so tight he'd quit feeling his fingers.

Sometimes they talked some silly-talk.

Then one Sunday the sheriff decided she'd marry a banker. The banker owned a railroad. The railroad led to Chicago. The sheriff liked Good Stuff so he told him himself, with whiskey, at the only saloon in town. "It'd be best for you if you left now," he said, and stood up quick and shuffled to the door, as if showing him the way.

Good Stuff pushed off his stool, the one he'd built, and turned to catch up, not knowing what he'd do, but the barkeep snatched his arm and said, "Hold on, you got free ones coming."

"I don't want no free ones."

"Can't say no to free ones," said the barkeep, and poured them out, one two three four. Looking copper in the light.

Good Stuff wouldn't drink. He sat on his stool and watched the barkeep watch him back.

Most everyone advised against their meeting one last time but they got together anyhow, by the creek. She looked like she'd been dying of dysentery for a week. She said they'd get accustomed to it. She said he could come to Chicago and track her down anytime he damn well wanted.

"By your new last name."

She pulled damp pages out from under her shirt, her hands shaking. "Your songs."

The first words he'd ever written down. She'd taught him how: the flip-sides all jammed up with practice-scribbles.

He pushed them back. "Our songs," he said. It was the most awful thing he could think to say, and also the best.

"HIS THIRD"

The Spanish don's daughter, descended from conquistadors, the most gorgeous woman him and everyone he knew had ever seen.

When California was being named, her granddaddies jumped up from Mexico with servants and gunmen, started planting and shooting, marrying, frying steaks, building floors and dancing on them. Way back they owned one-quarter of the coast.

They didn't own so much now but were rich and didn't like gringos, this being one of the reasons why Good Stuff's face got knocked in when they were found out in her room—he'd had time to cover her and hop the bed before the Spanish don's men floored him with a flurry of pistol-whipping. She'd watched— terrified, proud, and invincible, the same way she'd watched him undress her.

They hauled Good Stuff down the stairs, tossed him in the cellar, and took turns stepping on his face.

His boots and guitar had been left beneath her bed—a fancy thing, four-posted and perfumed. Her still on it.

The men bolted the cellar door and hurried upstairs. Company had come, other rich folks. A fiesta.

Good Stuff lay on the floor like something spilled from a sack. He couldn't hold all the hurting at the same time, so it dropped in pound by pound. Through the hurting he heard boots and heels and wood. Music too: horns and guitars, an accordion, many men singing with one voice. Muffled but magnificent.

Hearing this made him hot with a need to touch things. When he could stand up, he did. Blood ran down his neck, shoulders, and chest, shined out in trails from his trampled face. This was the biggest room he'd ever been in and there was plenty to touch: broken farm tools saved out for spare parts, crates of wine, jarred fruits and vegetables, empty bottles lined up in boxes. He grasped every object, rubbed every surface. He couldn't blink. He'd met her in the road. She was beautiful and he was beautiful, and they traded greetings in English and Spanish, and he played and sang. They both knew that what they were having had nothing to do with who they were, only where they were and how they were, right then, and this truth was as magnificent as the muffled music coming through the ceiling. She'd taken his hand and led him the whole way to the ranch.

Among the farm tools he found an old guitar. Two strings, the base cracked and rat-gnawed. He squeezed its neck. He rapped its frets.

None of this touching really felt like touching, so he started playing, which began to feel like something. His mouth opened and returned to singing without words, just the milky gargle of a bloodied throat:

Ooooh-haeeee, haeee, hauuuu.
Ooooh-haeee, haaoooh.
Haeee, hauuu.
Hauuuu.

The dancing upstairs stopped. The music too.

Ooooh-haeee, haaoooh.

The cellar door unbolted and groaned open. He walked through bleeding and playing, thickly singing his wordless song.

Haeee, hauuu.
Hauuuu.

Blood slickened the guitar's strings. Blood pattered into the sound hole.

He entered a bright hall twice as big as the cellar and crammed with colorful people. Still playing, he passed them in bare feet, dripping across the dancing floor. He couldn't tell which well-dressed gentleman was the Spanish don. All the faces were soft and well-bred, but pulled tight, shocked without wanting to show it. They looked like they lived sure lives except for maybe once a month.

The musicians smiled stunned smiles. One's face was switch-backed in half-open scars. Another stamped with an eyepatch. All of them stayed in place, held down.

Good Stuff walked through the adobe arch into the early evening. The Spanish don's many dogs did not pursue.

The daughter watched him leave the ranch at her window, from where she'd helped him climb in. The cradling range of mountains fading. The daughter wanting badly to be feeling worse than she did.

"THE NOWHERE DOGS"

When he'd get to whichever somewhere town, he'd sit outside the saloon in the dirt and wait for the nowhere dogs to find him.

Sick and old, infected, starved, abused, they'd shuffle up in dozens and take turns resting their muzzles on his boots. They begged to be touched. He'd oblige — he'd knead their necks and ears, their boils and sores and burrs, and the dogs, unfeeling even in their rawest wounds, turned their bodies to invite still more.

Then Good Stuff would open his mouth and sing the willing ones into easy dying.

Anyone who watched, men, women, children, lawmen, undertakers, outlaws, they'd weep, even if they didn't think they had it in them, the tears tugged into dry air. Then they'd pick up their dogs.

Good Stuff didn't ask but they'd pay in cake and bread, hats and boots, knives, polish, jugs. Never meat. Never lodging.

And on and on, and over, wordlessly crisscrossing the West, feeling carried.

"THE BODIES"

When Good Stuff got older he stayed put in Oklahoma.

When he stayed put, his wordless singing let him go. It swaggered down the road, a body wandering outside his body. Ungrasped, he felt heavy but firm. He felt the need to build.

"HIS FOURTH"

The radio.

Good Stuff, a creaky old man. His head a hundred shelves of memories of singing songs. He lived alone inside a stuffy rowhouse he'd mostly built himself. The Jackley boy, who lived just down the street, came by every Sunday afternoon to listen to him play because his parents, who he never disobeyed, declared it Christian duty.

The Jackley boy was scared of Good Stuff's crumpled brow and smashed-toad eyeballs, disgusted by the spit bubbles he blew when he spoke. But he'd sit on the porch, close his eyes, listen to the old man play from his rocking chair, and pretend the songs came from somewhere else. From the mountains, or whatever worlds stretched behind them, the worlds his daddy had explored.

When the boy showed up the first thing Good Stuff did was tell a love story the boy wouldn't understand. There was always music in the love story, and he'd cap it with a two-part saying:

"Music ain't the tool of the devil. The devil's the tool of the music."

"Music's made of love. But love ain't made of music."

"Music don't make the world smaller. Just makes you bigger."

Then he'd ask the Jackley boy to fetch his guitar, and he'd play and sing with words. He thought he'd miss the wordlessness more than he did. Mostly he thought of Sunday afternoons, of looking forward to them.

One Sunday morning Good Stuff woke and felt someone's arm laying on him heavily. His tired heart fluttered. Daring not to touch it, he kept his eyes shut, thankful to whoever had walked into his house and climbed into his bed and thrown his or her arm across him like a lover's. He felt the surging of an old and stupendous feeling. When that feeling crested an hour later, he looked. It was his own arm, as senseless as a ham.

He carried his arm all day like the thing still belonged to someone else, setting it down tenderly, rubbing the skin slowly. Good Stuff didn't get the feeling back until lunchtime. He found himself conflicted by his arm's return. He stood on the porch and got to thinking about what it might feel like to be someone else.

The Jackley boy came by. Before telling a love story, before playing, Good Stuff asked him what he did on the other days of the week when he wasn't here being so good-hearted visiting with an ugly old man.

The boy looked up from drawing stick animals in the porch-dust. "I like to listen to the radio."

The radio, who hadn't heard about the radio? Good Stuff knew the radio came from nowhere but at the same time from towers in Chicago. He knew something about Chicago. He patted the boy's little elbow and said, "Can you bring me a radio, son?"

"My daddy can." He sped straight home.

Mr. Jackley brought the radio over, the boy tagging excitedly along, wanting to help carry it, wanting to watch his daddy carry it. A dozen neighborhood kids saw Mr. Jackley hefting the beautiful bulky contraption down the street. They dropped their sticks and tops and jump ropes and followed, and before long were crowding up Good Stuff's porch, being noisy, roughhousing, too excited by the radio to get the willies from Good Stuff's misshapen face.

Mr. Jackley, a quiet veteran who'd served in the trenches, was sweating from exertion. He said good afternoon and removed his hat and set up the radio in the doorway. It was the size and shape of a liquor cabinet. The neighborhood kids all crouched low. A stillness spread among them. Good Stuff knew something big was about to happen but at the same time acknowledged that he'd never believe it until he saw it. Mr. Jackley turned the knob.

Music squeezed out as if from a magic room. The darkest room, the darkest magic. Good Stuff shivered, feeling it all over.

The neighborhood kids looked at the radio, through the radio, and into the invisible big-band orchestra. The musicians sounded a thousand miles away but also right next door and upstairs.

The Jackley boy grinned up at Mr. Jackley.

Mr. Jackley knew his boy was looking at him but he looked at Good Stuff.

Good Stuff wasn't looking anywhere.

When the song ended, Good Stuff flopped out of his rocking chair and onto his arm. His face jerked into pain and then straight out of it. The nearest kids hurried to help him up. He said, "Keep it playing!"

They listened to tunes until the news came on. All the neighbor-kids left.

Mr. Jackley guessed Good Stuff had broken his arm, and decided to call on the town doctor after he brought the radio back. He shook Good Stuff's hand lightly, put on his hat, got the radio ready, and lifted.

As he and his boy left the porch, Good Stuff said, "I been wrong all my life. Music don't make you feel more. Just makes you feel how much you keep missing."

Good Stuff raised his arm. He strummed the air with it. It was blue.

On the way home, the boy whispered to his dad, "But *what's* he been missing?"

Mr. Jackley set the radio on the street outside his house, needing but not wanting to rest before heaving it up the steps and through the front door. Inside, his wife cooked chili, pregnant again. Their blind cat napped under the porch. Mr. Jackley looked down at his son. His son looked back with love, even though he didn't know what love was or how it worked, where it came from, when it left you, how to know if it had stayed.

Mr. Jackley wanted to muster up enough to match this look. He couldn't.

He said, "Ask him next week."

They both looked over at Good Stuff's. The porch as empty as the street.

The boy got scared. "Can we ask him now?"

This Mr. Jackley could do.

They left the radio at the curb and walked back. The front door was open some.

What they couldn't see was that Good Stuff lay behind it, bunched up and on his head, one ear mashed to the floor. He'd fallen on his other arm. From this position he contemplated the many ways in which he could still be busted. A cause, he was certain, for thanks. The way he saw it, love had always come to him like a thing remembered. Known and new. And now the radio! It received what it was given, and what it received it gave. It gave to those who gathered round. What was far was now. The difference was, with enough money he could buy it, he could keep it close.

How close?

He tried to shake his arms. Both slept.

The boy knocked.

A church-like hush hugged the three of them.

The boy imagined Good Stuff's answers as songs that sounded sad but made you happy, and Mr. Jackley imagined daily ways to be on the other end of however many of his boy's loving looks were left, and Good Stuff imagined being one big wordlessness, being not what it came out of, but what came out.

Their quiet sparkled like warm static. They listened to it last.

Mutt-Face

Feeling puny, the mutt faced cowboy drove his truck through moonlight to the Mexican biker bar. He was a grubby Anglo with fat cheeks, otherwise lean, and he gunned along the country road with both windows down because neither would roll up. Every car he passed was packed with women. Some singing, big eyes pinched. His heart sputtered.

He hadn't been in a spell but the biker bar had stayed the same, stinking something fierce of bleach and lemons. Dark wood, dull light, rancheros howling. Everybody carrying on like they came from no place in particular, like they had no story other than the ones their bodies were saying right then and there with a mess of leaning, dancing, and laughing, with a mess of empty cans and bottles.

He took a stool and met his face in the mirror behind the bar. His mutt-face. Splotchy, chewed up, and smeared by the dopey grin he couldn't quit. He tugged his cowboy hat lower.

His orders kept the bartender moving. He had decided to drink himself big, so big that the bar cranked up and revolved around his bigness. So big that nagging things inside him, mostly memories, pretended to be puny. The bigness in him got bossy. It changed breeches.

Go on now, said the bossy bigness. Take a look-see.

He turned to his right and saw a large gal looking back, her lips like tomato halves, her cleavage like a canyon. Fill that canyon, said his bigness. The bar whirled behind her, flashing with female bodies. Bikes roared. Her face, a field aglow with makeup, was changing. He stared into her changing field, listening, imagining — filling up with bigness.

Then the biker beside her stepped up, the size of a jukebox, his eyes as dead and ugly as the Rio Grande, and the cowboy's bigness drained. The biker put on a pair of sunglasses like he was loading a pistol. Suddenly lonesome, the gal looked away.

The cowboy returned to his can of Tecate and added salt. He did not feel big. He felt the shoulder-tap he knew was coming, and when he turned, the biker slugged him off his stool. So many legs, some long and naked, and the biker, calm, was speaking, repeating himself. They stomped the cowboy's hat. Someone uncapped a saltshaker and poured it on his face, saying, "Qué sabroso," and they dragged him out the door and kicked him, but not enough to crack his bones.

He just lay there, feeling the moon on his neck. The door closed, muffling the laughter of women. Why you smiling at my woman, the biker had said. The bigness had no answer because the bigness skipped town and jumped the border.

When the burning in his eyes went out he pulled himself up and toward his truck, parked against a patch of prickly pear. Got no friends in there, he thought, meaning the bar.

Got no *friends,* shouted his bigness, from across the border it had jumped. It sipped a margarita, matter-of-factly. Women, neither.

The cowboy wiped gravel from his cheek and had himself a long look in the rearview: the irascible open-mouthed grin, the grin that was there whether he was puny or big, soused or sober, delusional, down in the dumps. The grin one saw instead of him. And now some broken teeth and a busted lip.

He wrenched the rearview off the windshield and tossed it out the window. After several tries, his truck started, wheezing.

The moon had risen from the mountains. Swollen and low,

it lit the valley. On the way to his crummy rented bungalow on the rural fringes of Mesilla, the cowboy bumped over the Rio Grande, smelled its sour and curdled reek through stuck-open windows. The smell was sad, so deeply sad that he thought for sure it'd kill or shrink his smile, but he touched the corners of his swollen lip and found them raised, idiotically defiant — a defiance without ground, without a resistance to properly define it, even. How about that. Sighing, he turned onto his country road and accelerated and smashed into a pecan tree.

The windshield folded closed, like a book. The moon came in and had its way with all the shattered glass, twinkling merrily. His nose dribbled blood. When thinking came back he thought: On purpose? Dogs were barking, hungry.

Then his door swung open. A crooked abuelita in a black dress snatched his hand, guided him out. She led and he followed, wobbling. Her grip was strong and dry. She didn't walk, exactly, she waggled her rump and floated, tugging him past a dried-up yard and blooming barrel cacti and withered scrub oaks and old standing engines, spaced out in her yard, looking like bird baths.

He watched her waggling rump and pretended she was fifty years younger.

A woman, clucked his bigness, before returning to the foreign bar.

Inside the adobe home the light was hard and orange. She took him through a sitting room cluttered with skinny shelves and curios: suffering saints and virgins, prayer candles, smiling suns and moons and skulls. From the carpet rose a thriftstore stink.

She sat him in the dining room, in a fold-up chair at a fold-up table. She floated, without clacking, across linoleum and into the kitchen. He dabbed his bloody nose with a sunny-colored cloth napkin. Plates clinked. Portraits adorned the walls, broad ones with fancy frames, spaced out in sequence. They had as their subject the same woman through time, from a self-assured sixteen-year-old to an alluring, busty thirty-something, ending on a pocked and silvery specimen of late middle age. The skin on the faces hardened as the cowboy followed the portraits from beginning to end; then softened as he backtracked, traveling through time with his gaze. Only the eyes and mouth were consistent: fierce, harried. The fierceness came from being harried. The mouth unsmiling, an iron bar.

The cowboy realized that these were not photographs, but paintings. He also realized he had lost his hat. "Nuts," he said, because his hair was thinning, and his hat was how he hid this fact from himself. The hat was a Stetson, which made him a cowboy. But that wasn't true, and boy, did he know it.

The abuelita reappeared, cradling a bowl with hands as big as oven mitts. In the bowl was a steaming hill of chile con carne. His place was set: fork, water glass.

He blinked hard, hoping to herd together his senses. "Thank you," he said, "this is a generous gesture, but I tell you, it's unnecessary. If you lend me your phone I'll use that phone to phone a friend and hitch a ride, and be on my way."

She shook her head, which was how she let him know she knew he had no friends. A motorcycle ripped by outside. He was still very drunk.

"Truck's a friend."

"Eat," she commanded.

He ate, hardly pausing to chew, and even cracked the knucklebones to slurp marrow. Soon the bowl was empty and he was full, feverishly warm. When she cleared his dish he tried to stand to help her. He couldn't. He'd been tied to the chair with twine.

She sat herself at the opposite end of the table, staring at him in the way that old folks have of trying to turn what they see into somewhere else, somewhere they've been before, way back.

The mutt-faced cowboy wriggled at his bonds. A pair of

hands clamped his shoulders, heavy ones. He smelled bleach and lemons and knew the man behind him to be the biker that had broke his teeth, the biker who had covered ugly eyes with sunglasses.

The abuelita opened her mouth and her voice was like a knife across a stone: "You were smiling when you were born, dogface."

"Please don't call me dogface."

"Dogs obey."

"All right: I'm a dogface."

The biker undid his bonds.

He stayed there, got used to it. Every morning he filled the old standing engines, which were, in fact, birdbaths for grackles. He dusted the curios on the shelves, straightened the portraits, and peeled potatoes. At night he slept on the porch swing out back near the chicken cages and dreamed of beautiful senoritas wrapped in immodest shawls made of darkness. Their lips shining, they'd touch his skin, join their bodies to his. At the end of these dreams the lights would go on and the shadow-shawls would disintegrate and the women would stand revealed as women from his family, sisters, aunts, and cousins, naked. It was embarrassing, but he woke with erections.

The abuelita fed him well and did his laundry. When he ate, she watched. Sometimes she licked her lips, and he was amazed that she had retained such powers of salivation. But he remained polite. Her mouth glistened, ashy gray.

Every day after lunch the cowboy would lay out on the same swing and have a nap, aiming to dream of senoritas he didn't know. But he never dreamed during naps, and when he woke in the late afternoon the biker would be standing beside him, smoking a cherry cigarillo and wearing shades. Dogs over the fence behind the chicken cages would be barking madly, keeping at it all day. The cowboy and the biker never said anything to each other, and on account of the biker always wearing shades the cowboy wasn't sure where the man was looking. At the Organ Mountains? The range was rocky and huddled, purple at the closing and opening of day. Its peaks looked like a gathering of unattractive women.

Its peaks are no such thing, said the bigness. They're teeth. People been eaten, there.

But the cowboy could now ignore the bigness. All this time he didn't think about his stomped Stetson or his thinning hair. He never thought about his dopey grin because there were no mirrors in the abuelita's house, only painted portraits. He didn't even think about being puny. Lean, satisfied, he spent time just considering, easy-like, how every day was made of parts and how every part followed the other. Then he'd fall asleep.

One month went by. After a lunch of enchiladas, the cowboy woke from his dreamless nap. A drag of a day, the mountains looking tired and dusty. Overworked women. The biker standing by, smoking, and for the first time he offered the cowboy a cigarillo.

The cowboy sat up, the bony knobs of his back rutting against the swing-slats. His face felt like the mountains looked. "Why not," he said, and realized those were the first words he'd said out loud in a month.

They were also the words he pretended to live by. An awful sadness poured on into him, taking the shape of the Rio Grande, surging in its sick and clotted way, all bigness on the far bank, impossible.

"Why you smiling at my woman," repeated the biker.

"At *everybody's* women," said the cowboy, "come from a family of them — moms, aunts, sisters, cousins, spinsters, ladies, widows, a fine and loving family, feeding me and dressing me and making me out to be something big, saying I could have anything and be anyone. Be anything and have anyone, boy! See the cities, they put them anywhere!" He licked his lips. They were sweet with artificial cherry, dry with hot smoke. "So I got to leaving Georgia. Was fixing to be anyone and have anyone without them, and the women I knew gave me blessings and bank accounts and pieces of pie for the road. Next thing I know I'm turning my back to weepy goodbyes and blasting through Alabama and Mississippi and Louisiana, seeing cities, wild ones, and landing in Texas, buying boots and a hat, talking different, working orchards and farms, nuts, tomatoes, tripping through canebrake, tearing my breeches, and always every night phoning up my family women so they can feel good reminding me: *Be anyone and have anyone, boy!*" The cowboy laughed hard and short, like a man who had stepped on the face of death. "And now I'm in New Mexico. Picking pecans. Making up my life with all them womenfolk out of earshot."

The biker nodded his huge head, without a doubt looking at the mountains. He offered the cowboy a second cigarillo. And because the cowboy had just lied like crazy, lies on top of lies on top of lies, puny, blatant, true-blue lies, this action struck the cowboy as the kindest thing anyone had ever done for him—the manful, wordless offering of a smoke, no questions, no calling-out—and the cowboy was crying when he said, "I can't light this goddamn thing."

All the dogs had shut up. The biker helped him light his second cigarillo. "Why'd your woman look so lonesome," asked the cowboy, trying to cough the thickness from his throat.

The biker pointed to the swing where the cowboy had been sleeping and waking up in shame. "That's where I was born," he said. He pointed to the rotten fence, the one that screened the silent dogs. "That's where mi madre died." He holstered his pointing hand in the pocket of his leather jacket. "This is where I decided to buy my first bike."

"I get you," said the cowboy, weeping hard. "You're just like me but you're nothing like me, to boot." His face sagged, but still smiled.

"Nothing like you," corrected the biker.

The cowboy pulled at the corners of his mutt-faced mouth, tugging them down. It had no effect.

"Ask mi abuelita," said the biker.

The cowboy went inside and asked the abuelita how to stop smiling so much. She'd been stirring a pan of chicken feet.

She took off her apron and put down her wooden spoon. Not smiling, she took him by the hand and led him out of the kitchen, past the portraits, to her bedroom. The room was black and shuttered, one red candle blazing. She pushed him firmly to the bed and puffed out the flame.

In the darkness she became a body builder. He'd never felt so puny in all his life, and as the bed squealed beneath them, all his family women filled a hall inside his head, a hall he rushed right through because they didn't care where he was going. They really didn't. He went on weeping. She heaved him through a sequence of positions, grunting.

Then he understood that he'd been visiting the abuelita like this every night while half-asleep. All the senoritas had been her. What's more, it'd been pretty good. He renewed his efforts.

"Adios," she said, when she'd led him back to the front door.

She was smiling. He wasn't. But he felt all right, considering.

He walked to the pecan tree that had caught his truck, where the vehicle waited, crumpled. He brushed the seat of glass and dust. Someone had left a mound of cans on the mat. A breeze hissed through the shattered windshield and touched his lips, not his teeth.

The truck felt old, older than the abuelita. Maybe because there was no mirror to meet himself inside of.

To his surprise, it started.

Five Episodes of White-Hat Black-Hat

I. BAD NEWS FROM OVER BIG MOUNTAIN; OR, THE HERO IS CALLED TO ADVENTURE

The white-hat cowboy sat on a caved-in well at the edge of town. A ways away, near mountains, the wind was bored with sheets of dust. It was noon. The sun had put its foot down on everything.

Waiting, the white-hat cowboy tried to look like he wasn't. He tried to look like no one living could recall a time when anything could come for anyone. He jiggled his toes inside his boots.

Noon stayed right where it was. The wind yawned.

The white-hat cowboy tilted up the brim of his white hat and looked straight into the sun. His vision burst into a silvered burning landscape — a field of heaven-fire, angels flailing at the melting gate, the clouds all up in smoke — a holy burning so hot he heard it, barely. He tilted down his white hat. He fell asleep.

The pony express rider rode in from the mountains. He was also asleep. His horse, starving, trotted past the white-hat cowboy. The mail in the saddlebags had a lot to say and couldn't wait to say it. When opened, it would tell of the men shot, women kidnapped, cattle rustled, and gold stolen by the black-hat cowboy and his gang of outlaws. It would tell of the tribesmen ambushed by soldiers and the soldiers ambushed by tribesmen and the slaves running from slave-owners and the slave-owners running after slaves. It would tell the white-hat cowboy, I am a monster.

The white-hat cowboy would say it wasn't so.

The mail would say it was.

The white-hat cowboy would get up to sit on something else.

II. A POWWOW AT THE DOODLEBUG RANCH;
OR, THE HERO RECEIVES UNEXPECTED AID

The white-hat cowboy sat on a caved-in fence at the edge of the sheriff's ranch. A ways away, near mountains, settlers played a slow game with last year's farmland. It was afternoon. The sun dipped in and out of napping.

Bored, the white-hat cowboy tried to look like he wasn't. He tried to look like nothing had been, was, or would be more important than what was sure to happen next. He rolled his spurs against a splintered post.

Afternoon dozed facedown. The settlers went in for water.

From the sheriff's ranchhouse came the sheriff, the sheriff's niece from back east, and the teenage orphan. They moseyed through parched grasses to where the white-hat cowboy sat. The sheriff rode a horse, a very old one. It had swallowed all its teeth.

The white-hat cowboy stood up on the caved-in fence right on the spot where the black-hat cowboy and his gang of outlaws had busted in last night. They'd shot the sheriff's ranch hands, kidnapped the sheriff's daughters, rustled the sheriff's cattle, and stolen the sheriff's cash.

The white-hat cowboy shook his head.

The sheriff attempted to wink in a manly way, which made him look even older than his very old horse. The sheriff's niece from back east blushed on account of feeling expected to, and though she longed for it, she felt no love for the white-hat cowboy, whether there'd be a baby or not. The teenage orphan wanted badly to be anyone else. He just about cried.

Together they waited for the white-hat cowboy to speechify. The white-hat cowboy said, "Well, shoot."

Together they understood him to want to mean, Where would you be without me?

The white-hat cowboy unbuckled his gunbelt as importantly as he could and handed it to the teenage orphan, who dropped it. Both sixguns went off in the dirt. The teenage orphan pissed his britches.

The white-hat cowboy unpinned his deputy badge as officially as he could and handed it to the sheriff, who in reaching for it fell off his saddle. The very old horse snorted and stomped and crushed the sheriff's arms and legs. The sheriff shat his britches.

The white-hat cowboy took off his white hat as tragically as he could and set it on the head of the sheriff's niece from back east. The brim dropped to her chin, hiding her face. She sat in the dirt and clutched her belly. Her dress darkened with sudden blood and what wouldn't be a baby.

The white-hat cowboy held up his pants with his hands. He didn't know what to give next. A ways away, the settlers waved at him. Without his white hat he looked like one of them.

III. THIN WALLS IN THE WHOREHOUSE;
OR, THE HERO CROSSES THE THRESHOLD

The white-hat cowboy sat on the edge of a caved-in bed at the only whorehouse in town. A ways away, near the door, a whore was bored with makeup at the basin. It was night. The moon had opened its little mouth.

Satisfied, the white-hat cowboy tried to look like he wasn't. He tried to look like there were things he wanted more than this, things that whatever he had was in the way of. He put on his white hat. It was all he wore.

Night licked its lips. The whore closed up her makeup. She said, "Any news from anywhere that ain't here?"

The white-hat cowboy touched the wall to his right. It wobbled with musical grunts and creaks and groans.

She said, "Songs? Jokes? Yarns?"

The white-hat cowboy touched the wall to his left. It wobbled with the voice of a storyteller and the laughter of his listeners. The laughter came from many men and women and was of as many kinds: wholesome and cruel, kind and filthy, mad, lonesome, loving. The story he couldn't understand a word of. The voice was of one kind, a kind he didn't know, but he knew to who it belonged. It belonged to the black-hat cowboy.

The white-hat cowboy was crying. He tried to make his crying look like joyful participation in the misfortunes of the world.

"Oh," said the whore, let-down. "You ain't never left."

IV. CAPTURED BY OUTLAWS; OR, THE HERO FACES TRIALS

The white-hat cowboy sat on the caved-in cactus he was tied to at the edge of the outlaws' camp. A ways away, near the fire, the black-hat cowboy and his gang of outlaws were bored with bags of cash. It was sunset. The sun, drunk and still drinking, shared what it had with the clouds and mountains.

Relieved, the white-hat cowboy tried to look like he wasn't. He tried to look like there were fights to fight. He swallowed some of his teeth.

The sunset ordered another round. The black-hat cowboy whooped and took a shit into the fire.

One by one the black-hat cowboy's outlaws whooped and took shits into the fire.

Blushing, the white-hat cowboy hid his face beneath the brim of his white hat. He couldn't understand anything his captors said, did, or were.

The black-hat cowboy and his gang of outlaws sang songs and danced dances and thrust their dicks into the fire, and when the sun passed out, they stuffed the white-hat cowboy and the caved-in cactus he was tied to into a sack in such a way that his head poked out. They slung the sack onto a horse and rode to town. On the way they set fire to tribal villages, shot up settlers' covered wagons, and dynamited passenger trains. In town they robbed a bank. On the way back they kidnapped five gals. They agreed to throw the gals into the fire.

The sack the white hat cowboy was stuffed into had become wet with blood, his blood and the blood of others. He felt light on the outside and heavy on the inside, a bit like a lie you'd tell a child.

The outlaws stripped the gals. The gals let them. Their skin flashed bright in the firelight. The white-hat cowboy didn't want to watch, but did.

The first didn't see him on her way into the fire.

The second did but didn't know him.

The third knew him but pretended not to.

The fourth pretended to appreciate his being there. She waved.

The fifth was pregnant.

V. TO THE TOP OF NO-RETURN PEAK; OR, THE HERO RETURNS

The white-hat cowboy sat on a torn-up bloody sack on a caved-in cave on a mountain peak. A ways away, near town, black ash and old coals were bored with the ruins of settlers' homes, barns, and fields. It was sunrise. The sun hadn't slept at all.

Moved, the white-hat cowboy tried to think he wasn't. He tried to think that the only feeling worth feeling was bored black ash and old coals. This thought, he acknowledged, was a lie, the lie he kept coming back to, the lie that led like a rope to where he was. All the lie tied him to was itself. His limbs were broken, he'd pissed and shat his britches, and beside him lay somebody's baby. The baby was dead.

The sunrise didn't look so good but put on a brave face.

The wind took off the white hat cowboy's hat. It journeyed down the mountain while he watched.

Fourteen Cowboys
by the Fire

Fourteen cowboys by the fire, laying out and crouching, stinking. The herd behind them settling down. The fire eating what brush and wood they'd gathered.

When they'd gathered, their dogs had found a dead man in a parched ravine. All could see he'd lately been alive, yet to be stripped of boots and belt. He'd had his head broke in. The stained rock sat homey in a nearby bush, a speckled egg in a nest.

And now no moon, no wind, no words. Faint starlight on the sleeping herd, on the many headless mountains.

Adamson thought, Why not use a knife?

Martinez thought of the white man who'd come at him with a saucepan.

Hunson, Jones, and Cloud Horse, older than the others, thought of the wars.

Miller thought of the red men he'd shot one by one from his high perch on a hot rock.

McWhorter of the red man he'd shot six times when the man had turned to wash his face in the hotel basin.

Gomez of the black man he'd beaten with a chair.

Bauer and Metzer of the black man they'd thrown into the poisoned well.

Bohland of the brown man he'd hog-tied, roped to his saddle-horn, and dragged at a gallop over cacti and ocotillo and ashes.

Gaines of the brown man he'd bound to a tree and mutilated and abandoned, the red man he'd bound to a chair in a cave and

burned alive, and the white man he'd bound and raped and stran-
gled in a whorehouse.

Whistling Pete of the yellow man he'd smothered on a cot in
a cell.

Redondo of the dozens of white, brown, and black men
that he and others had driven a stampede into, scrambling and
screaming men who could not then or now be counted. He tried
again to count them. Then the women, then the children.

Redondo nudged a hissing log.

Whistling Pete pinched one nostril and noodled snot through
the other.

Gaines belched in the middle of a belch.

Bohland stood to stretch his back.

Bauer passed Metzer a pouch of tobacco.

Gomez cleaned his teeth with grass.

McWhorter spat into his hand and worked it under his pants.

Miller combed his hair, his moustache, and his sideburns, and
then his sideburns, his moustache, and his hair.

Cloud Horse, Jones, and Hunson, side by side and on their
backs, faked hard sleep.

Martinez laughed a little.

And Adamson drew his knife, just to see the fire jump onto
the blade.

NEW WEST

Big Lonesome Middles

MORNING IN NEW MEXICO

Before the cowboy woke his body did. He'd slept on her roof.

His body sat up, pushed aside the stinking horseblankets, and stood. The sun hunched behind the mountains, scheming the sky into pink and purple mapwork. He came to his body as his body saw the smashed blue faces of the backlit mountains, mountains he'd until this month only known from their other side. Their Texas side. Their fat cows and worn horses and clever men, men he'd come to know like he'd come to know horses.

What he saw from the roof he didn't own. But he couldn't kick feeling that this was most of what he'd traded for: the pecan orchard's miserable trees jammed into wet ditches, a junkyard plugged with rusted hulks, an unplowed onion field. Her uncle's four adobe bungalows. Her brother's truck. The long lick of shriveled road.

He stepped to the roof's graveled edge, to the scrub oak he'd climbed last night. He slapped its scaly bark. To him the smell of the morning was the smell of the state, rich and pregnant and old, older than man but nowhere near as old as woman. She would be in bed. Her dark body creasing sheets, her short legs long, her black hair brown with light. She never went to bed in clothes, even when she'd strike him, when he'd shout her down. Already they took turns playing roles and pretending roles were who they were.

When he was on the job Boot Slaw had only ever said one thing every day, that you were wrong about a horse on purpose.

He rode the scrub oak down and landed with a crunch. He kept his back to the door. She'd tossed his pack into the bed of her brother's truck. The windows gleamed red, all four tires flat.

He left his pack where it lay and took to the road's tongue, mute and parallel to mountains.

MORNINGS IN NEW MEXICO

When he'd left the job on the mountains' Texas side and traded his gear and two guitars to Bad Man McWhorter, she'd begun to make tortillas every morning. The smell of them shrank him.

She knew this. She loved this. She spread their tortillas with what they'd borrowed or bought, queso and chile, butter and beans, eggs, onions, cilantro, salt, and the plates she put before him pulled him from his body's edges, cinching him closer to a center he couldn't know at any other time. He'd slouch, mouth cowing open, eyelids thickening. A train of tiny sighs.

She loved that although this wasn't him this was in him.

He loved that she loved the effect for the effect and not for its causes, whatever they might be.

They both loved that they could love this no matter who they'd be that afternoon, no matter where they'd been the night before.

NIGHTS IN TEXAS

Boot Slaw was so big that others boasted for him. The men he worked with would tall-tell how The Unbeatable But Not Unbearable Boot Slaw had shouted downed cows back to standing and broken wild horses by bare-hand strangling them blue and plucked diving hawks from the air to kiss their killing beaks, and more astounding still, with selfless concern for the nation's future, had from scores of respectable married ladies fathered herds of big-fisted boys who in babyhood spurned milk to drink ground chuck.

To such yarns Boot Slaw would laugh-shout, "The whole truth is more big."

In fact he stood a few hands shy of seven foot, his heaped-up arms and shoulders set for grabbing hard and crushing slow. His face did its best to look like a fool boy's. He could eat until you begged him to stop and throw anything farther than anyone and his boulder-in-a-gully laugh you felt in your boots. He wasn't trail boss but the trail boss did what he said if he said it. He was point-rider.

When night curtained and the first shift of night-riders saddled up to circle the herd, Boot Slaw would stand at the fire shirtless and declare his intent to wrestle. He'd pace, making rodeo clown faces, and stop in front of somebody he hadn't got to yet. He'd challenge that somebody by clamping his hand to their shoulder.

The cowboy, older only than the calves, had watched nightly with fear and hope as the one man challenged declined with a laugh. Boot Slaw was too big to take refusal personally. He'd sit down and haul a shirt back on. All returned to telling yarns and sharing bottles. The cowboy would play guitar and try more than ever to feel the notes in ways he knew he couldn't.

Those nights the cowboy's body wouldn't hand him sleep. It wanted more than what it had.

Those days the cowboy rode drag at the herd's noisy backside, breathing the dust and the stink. He'd prod the sick, the weak, the scared. More than once while doing so he tumbled from his saddle into shitpies.

Then their night arrived: Boot Slaw stopped his pacing at the cowboy. He loomed like a landscape, too big to remember right.

The hand came down.

The cowboy felt it clap into his heels. Boot Slaw waited,

high and broad, grinning. Everybody watched. The cowboy accepted the challenge with a wild surprise tackle—endless acres had opened inside him, unplowed, aflame—and his ferocity was such that he toppled Boot Slaw at first go, slamming him flat into a stack of gear.

But not at second, third, or seventh go, as every night that last week on the job they crashed snarling into brushpiles and potracks, tripping over their reclining fellows who hee-hawed and ya-hooed from the holes in their fire-slashed faces. When he got his grip, which he always did, Boot Slaw flapped the cowboy around like a hide he'd cut himself.

Between rounds Boot Slaw sang the songs of his old country and shadowboxed in stances no one had ever seen.

Between rounds the cowboy found his arms and legs, even when he lost, which was every go but the first.

AFTERNOON IN NEW MEXICO

The cowboy trudged the road into the afternoon. He'd trudged this road twice before on his way to Bad Man McWhorter's to trade his gear and two guitars for the one sad purse of cash he'd brought back to his woman, the woman he right now walked away from. Although he didn't carry anything this time, he didn't feel unburdened—the sun had been doubling him all day, adding arms to his arms and legs to his legs, the limbs rooting in and rising from his back in a doughy sprouting. It was as though he'd been forced to bed himself and lay together afterwards, awake.

He figured if he'd only feel this way from here on out he wouldn't be any good to a woman or a horse or a man like Bad Man McWhorter again, and so what.

What good was being any good?

Boot Slaw's answer, he imagined, would be to pretend to take a swing at him.

The cowboy reached Bad Man McWhorter's stretch of fence. He set doubled hands on a post alive with painted grasshoppers. Every one of them leaped. There grazed the horse that was once his horse, at home with other horses that once were other men's horses. More awful yet was what rose behind them: the stables, the barn, the house, all newly stained. They had the look of having always been there.

The cowboy's head doubled.

The cowboy's heart doubled.

The more of him there was the more he felt he could take. He hugged his shoulders with his arms and his shoulders with his arms. With both heads he looked at the mountains. Seen this way they were one thing with one side, the mountains' side. Mountains knew how to make up their minds.

Right then Bad Man McWhorter loped into view from the awful stables, slow as smoke. He whistled all the horses back. The horse that was once the cowboy's trotted, each leg doing something different, independent but unified, balanced in one body.

The cowboy recalled when he and the woman he walked away from had last ridden that horse together. This hurt more than recalling when he and the woman had met in town, by the trough. He wiped both his sweaty brows.

When Bad Man McWhorter reappeared it was to lean on the rifle that was once the cowboy's rifle. He stood many yards away but his face flew red and warty, a bloated flag. He thumbed at himself.

The cowboy's arms helped his arms heft himselves onto the fence, where his legs wrapped legs to sit tight. His hearts hammered hearts.

Bad Man McWhorter laughed, a grainy cackle. Behind him his three daughters stepped out of the awful barn. They were lean and muddy with animals' faces. They held big tools. Bad

Man McWhorter jigged around the rifle, wheezing, jubilant. His wife pushed through the back door of the awful house, her apron brushed with blood and flour. Unlike the awful stables, barn, and house, she had the look of having had it worse than this.

The cowboy's heads shook yes to her.

She stood as still as a split rock.

The cowboy's heads traded glances: one hopeful, one hopeless.

Bad Man McWhorter stopped jigging. He'd seen his women.

Then the women went away.

The cowboy fell off the fence and into himself, road-side.

Cowgirl

Cowgirl, born of a beef cow, lands with a squelch in the mud. Fall is beaming, bright, a small cold sunrise. She steams.

The cow cowgirl is born of moos, saying: Ours?

Cowgirl, facedown, does not turn over.

Other beef cows look.

Cowgirl is a human person female girl. Not a baby, not a child, not a grown-up. Naked.

The cow cowgirl is born of bends to sniff her.

Ours?

Cowgirl turns onto her back. She clears the mud from her face.

The cow cowgirl is born of is afraid.

Cowgirl is afraid, and then she isn't. She sits up. The cow licks her hard. Against each lick, cowgirl feels herself, her hot skin and blood, her muscles and bones, her packed-tight inner organs. At her center twists a need to move. She isn't sure if she should speak.

The cow licks cowgirl's mouth.

You are not my mother, says cowgirl.

The cow moos. Her udder sags, swollen rich.

Cowgirl rolls away, in the mud and feed and shit, layering herself, making a stinking hide. It spreads in smears and lumps. It crusts in the early light.

The sun, done rising, retires its red and golden banners.

Cowgirl stands. Flies outline her. The farm's low buildings

stamp clear shadows. She walks to the fence. It's wooden, slatted, pricked with shot. She touches it, amazed.

Don't, says a young man.

The young man has the face of a woman. He's standing in a shed, holding a loop of calving chains. He's embarrassed.

Cowgirl is embarrassed, and then she isn't. She squats. She pisses and shits.

The young man tries to look like he knows what to say to that and is just about to say it.

Cowgirl stoop-steps between the fence and crosses a country road and walks into a field of tall green crops. Their shade is cold and deep, near-night. Their low leaves brush her in dew. She comes to a trampled place where slashed light enters. She stands in a slice of it. Through her mud-hide, she feels her hands and face, her neck, her trunk and torso, her privates, her legs and feet—a springiness, a scrappiness—she feels joy, and then she doesn't. The light she stands in dims and slants. Do her feelings come from the inside, then move out, or do they come from the outside, then move in? An answer, she guesses, will help her know what to do and say, when she should be what to who. The light sharpens. She's thirsty, hungry. She walks the field of tall green crops until it breaks into a field of short green crops, almost short enough to see over, which she walks until it ends in a sloppy garden. Small plants bulge red, green, and purple vegetables. She eats them. She folds wet leaves and drinks in sips. She walks the garden until it ends in a driveway to a farmhouse.

The driveway is lined with tables stacked in decorations, appliances, tools, toys. Items too big for the tables lean against them.

She touches a bicycle, amazed.

Wait, say two old men.

The two old men sit at the driveway's end in lawn chairs, dented cashboxes in their laps. Both are alarmed.

Cowgirl is alarmed, and then she mounts the bicycle.

The two old men look at her like she can't know what she's doing.

Her fingers link into the handles' grooves. She can know how to ride, she feels, or she can not know how to ride. She can sit straight and grip right or she can tilt too far and topple. She knows who she should be to this bicycle. Her butt fits the seat.

Come here, say the two old men.

She pushes off   she rides down the driveway to a country road, the one she crossed before, and takes it, biking between fields and farms and homes. The breeze she makes by moving laps at her. Her mud-hide dries and flakes. Thrilled, she passes fields of farms like the farm she left, their tagged cows standing and sitting and chewing, and she passes fields of crops like the fields she walked, their long rows ripening or withering, and she passes fields of homes, their doors and windows shut. The country road curves downhill and past a big wooden sign and into the main street of a small town.

A group of middle-aged men stand around their trucks at a gas station, smoking. The young man with the face of a woman is there, perched on a tractor, sighing and shaking his head. From his shoulder hangs the loop of calving chains.

Cowgirl brakes in the street. It's noon already, shadows skinny under everything.

The young man gasps.

Look at that, say the middle-aged men.

The middle-aged men are interested.

Cowgirl is interested, then alarmed, then embarrassed. Then none of it.

The middle-aged men put out their cigarettes and spit out their chew. They approach. They move slowly, smiling big.

Where's your mother? say the middle-aged men. Who's your father?

The young man with the face of a woman waves, trying to look like he knows what he means by it. The calving chains slide off with a jingle and a crash.

Cowgirl shifts from the seat to put her feet on the pavement. She feels bad for the young man. He can't seem to speak. He touches his chest with one hand, and then the other, but he doesn't know where to go from there.

She looks at her hands on the bicycle's handlebars. She feels bad for herself.

Cars have stopped in the street, both lanes backed up.

The middle-aged men come close. They smell like the insides of places.

You are not my fathers, says cowgirl.

She pedals away. The middle-aged men rush to their trucks, and the young man scoops up the chains and boards his tractor, and together they roar into the road, engines ripping, tires barking, and cowgirl, pursued, turns down a side street, across a sidewalk, over a driveway, through a yard, and onto a path between two houses, where she stops beneath windows she's too short to see into. In one house, a big-sounding man laughs alone, laughing himself to more laughter, bumping through a maze of it. Cowgirl wheels her arms and laughs, but it doesn't bring her anywhere, it's only practice. In the other house, a different voice: a big-sounding woman talks to herself, and at the same time, to someone else. She's asking questions. The questions are advice. Cowgirl moves along, half-riding, barely pedaling. She talks to herself, and at the same time, to someone else, saying, Do I come from myself? Do I come from outside myself? Do I need to know? Do I need new questions? and this isn't practice, this is a maze — rows and shadows, corners and voices — How can I know where to go from here? — the wind — and she's biking fast, she's biking hard, she gasps — she slams into a bench and flips over it and lands in grass on her back.

She's in a weedy park. A nearby group of boys is throwing a football, not really trying to catch it. They're looking to bang each other around. They stop.

They say, You're weird.

She sits up.

You don't look right, one says.

What happened to your wiener, says the one with the football, pointing at her crotch.

Girls don't have them, stupid.

I'm insulting her, stupid.

Cowgirl stands. She says, Don't.

One of them shoves her and she shoves back, and another shoves her from behind and she falls, and they take her bicycle and dash off laughing and hooting and yelling, except for one. He asks if he can help her.

Wait, she says.

She gets up on her own. She looks at her body.

He is enchanted.

Cowgirl is enchanted, and then she isn't.

I want to give you something, he says.

He jiggles out of his sweatshirt and his sweatpants. They'll fit, he says, handing them over, happy in his undershirt, in his underpants.

She puts them on. They don't fit. They smell like the space she stood in between houses.

The boy is looking at her. He's seeing time, time together, his time and her time, the two of them in every place he knows. He's hoping that she'll start looking at him in the same way.

She sees this. Come here, she says.

He can't seem to find himself.

Look at that, she says.

He's blinking and swallowing and shaking.

She touches his hand. His whole body quivers, tightens.

Where is your mother, she says.

Cleaning houses. She cleans houses.

Who is your father?

Marge. I mean Frank! Frank.

She isn't looking at him how he's looking at her. He's disappointed, she notices, but hopeful.

She smiles big.

He smiles big and sweats.

You don't look right, she says.

The boy points at a worn-out house on the other side of the park, prepares to say something, and is hit in the back of the head with a football—his glasses jump off his face, he stumbles to one knee.

The boys cheer from the street. They chant a nickname: girlie man, girlie man, girlie man!

I have to go, the boy says to cowgirl, crying.

Cowgirl skips across the park, around a corner, and up a hill. Bright leaves swish underfoot. It's late afternoon. Between low shadows shoot copper-golden corridors. She jumps in and out of their light. She scratches mud from her face and she shakes mud from her hair, twirling in a shower of clumps and crumbs. She'll go where she goes! She puts her hands in the sweatshirt's front pocket and finds an action figure, a squinting cowboy. Its hat is fused to its head. She flicks at the hat-head seam and walks between two slanted gates and into a graveyard. Headstones lean in rows, like houses, like crops. She slaps a few with the action figure, an attempt to unhat or unsquint it. Two bicycles are stacked against a tree. The tree is tall, a burst of red leaves, a burst of black roots. She peeks around its trunk.

Two teen boys slouch near a bush, drinking whiskey from a water bottle.

She can tell them what to do, she thinks, and they will do it. They can carry chains. They can stand at fences and sit in chairs.

They can wait, and stare, and move in groups, and drive trucks and tractors, and hit boys in the head with the things they're playing with, and take away whatever it is that the girls they meet are using to get to places.

Imagining this, cowgirl is disappointed. But hopeful.

One of the teen boys is impatient, the other bored.

Cowgirl, impatient, bored, leans out of her hiding spot. The teen boys see her but pretend they don't. She edges closer, behind a memorial sculpture, a chalice on a pedestal. The chalice is big enough to serve her in.

The impatient teen boy says, Why does it take girls so long to get anywhere!

They want to look good, says the bored one.

They already usually do!

Cowgirl climbs the sculpture. She hunkers in the chalice.

Although the teen boys gesture like the middle-aged men from the gas station, their voices squeak closer to those of the boys from the park. They drink from the bottle, pretending not to grimace, and they talk sex, pretending to have talked sex with people who've had it. They discuss where dicks can be put. They discuss where they've seen dicks put on the internet. The impatient one waves a condom.

She's been around, he says, putting it back in his wallet.

The bored one shrugs. He rolls a cigarette on a tabled headstone.

Cowgirl stands, revealed. You're weird! she says.

The teen boys discuss vaginas and buttholes and breasts.

Cowgirl grips the rim of the chalice. She's blinking and swallowing and shaking. She wants to force the teen boys to stop pretending that she isn't there, and then she doesn't. But this "doesn't" isn't like the other doesn'ts—it isn't the easy opposite of "does." It's just as loaded with longing.

The afternoon lengthens, dulls.

Two teen girls arrive. One has a paper bag, the other a spar-kly purse. Both wear makeup. Their faces float and glow.

Who the fuck are you? says the one with the bag.

The one with the purse says, Are you lost?

The teen boys pretend they've just seen cowgirl.

She seems all right, says one.

Whatever, says the other. Sit.

The teen girl with the bag sits. She crinkles it open and passes out hamburgers. She gulps whiskey, glaring at cowgirl. She's angry and confused.

Cowgirl is angry and confused.

The teen girl with the purse approaches the sculpture's pedestal and looks up at cowgirl. She's concerned.

Cowgirl is concerned and angry and confused.

The concerned teen girl says, Where are you from?

Where is she *from* from? says the angry and confused teen girl.

The bored teen boy, still chewing, unwraps another hamburger. He makes an indifferent mumble.

Oh please, like it doesn't matter, says the angry and confused teen girl. She's probably from some fucked-up country.

Are you okay? says the concerned teen girl.

Cowgirl says, I want to give you something.

The concerned teen girl winces out a smile.

In the smile, cowgirl sees time, time together, her time and the teen girl's time, the two of them on farms and in fields, taking roads and streets and alleys, finding bicycles and riding them, finding boys and shoving them, skipping and twirling and practice-laughing and putting advice-questions to girls in chalices in graveyards.

Cowgirl sees the concerned teen girl seeing that she's seeing this.

The concerned teen girl is sad.

By the bush, the bored teen boy kisses the angry and con-fused teen girl. They grab at each other's crotches. They roll out of sight.

Cowgirl offers the squinting action figure.

The impatient teen boy touches the sad teen girl's shoulder. She's crying.

It's okay, he says, but it comes out sounding like, Is this im-portant?

She needs help! We have to help her!

Cowgirl starts crying.

The sad teen girl says, Want to come down?

Cowgirl doesn't move.

Okay, says the impatient teen boy. His impatience becomes patience. He stands on the pedestal. Let's go, come on.

Cowgirl becomes patient.

Careful, says the sad teen girl.

The patient teen boy motions. I'm helping you.

Cowgirl says, I have to go now.

Yes, he says, and reaches for her.

Cowgirl strikes him in the face with the action figure—he throws up his arms and falls—the sad teen girl screams—cow-girl scrambles down the other side of the sculpture and sprints through the graveyard, sad and concerned and angry and con-fused and screaming, and she scales a fence and crosses a road and enters a field, it's a farm, the sun is setting all over it, stack-ing bricks of color and breaking them, and she darts into an open barn where she passes stables and troughs and an old woman cur-ry-combing a big horse, and she ducks under a bench.

She listens to the curry comb whisk the big horse. She stops screaming.

The old woman says, Would you like to hear a story?

Cowgirl would.

The curry comb begins to whisk the big horse in a different way. The old woman tells a story about a little horse, named Little Horse, who runs away from her mother and father. Little Horse wanders the countryside, thinking that the land is home, finding that the land is foreign. The longer that Little Horse is away from her mother and father, the more she misses them, and the more she misses them, the more ashamed she feels about returning to them.

Cowgirl is now sitting on the bench.

The old woman dandy-brushes the big horse. She's watching cowgirl but pretending not to.

It's okay, says cowgirl, and it comes out sounding like, This is important.

The old woman tells a story about a small horse, named Small Horse, who's never met her mother or father. She wanders the countryside, thinking that the land is answers, finding that the land is questions. Small Horse meets animals who invite her to join their families—deer, raccoons, bears, squirrels, skunks, wolves—but to all she says, No thank you. The more animals she meets, the more different she feels from them. Then she meets an old horse, named Old Horse. Instead of inviting her to join her family, Old Horse invites her in for dinner.

The old woman is now sitting next to cowgirl. She touches cowgirl's hand.

Cowgirl's whole body quivers, tightens.

What do you think? says the old woman.

Together they walk out of the barn and toward a house. It's dark. The moon rises, a bleary red stone. In the driveway a middle-aged man grunts, heaving crates out of the bed of a scratched-up truck. He stops what he's doing to stare at cowgirl.

Careful, says cowgirl.

He leaves the crates where they are and gets in the scratched-up truck and starts it.

The old woman leads cowgirl into the house, where there

are many of the things that were on the tables in the old men's driveway. Here their arrangement is more harmonious. The light is dense and muffled. Between everything rolls a thickness of smell: warmth, bodies, food. A square table is being set by a young woman. She's pleased to see cowgirl.

Cowgirl stares, unsure.

The old woman leads cowgirl into the kitchen, where a middle-aged woman is knifing into a beef roast, wedging it open to check its color. She's pleased too.

Cowgirl stares.

The old woman leads cowgirl through the kitchen and into a bathroom, where she helps her into a tub, undresses her, scrubs her, rinses her, dries her, puts her in a dress, and gathers her hair into a ponytail.

You're brave, she says.

Cowgirl says, Whatever.

Come out when you're ready, says the old woman, closing the door behind her.

Cowgirl stands on the toilet and looks out the window. The middle-aged man and his scratched-up truck are gone. She sits, guiding her dress. A change moves through her—an inside-outing, an outside-ining—a stopping and a starting and a stopping. She touches her body: the beginnings of breasts. Her skin shines. She imagines the most important place inside herself. The place, she whispers, that's me. The place that I mean when I feel or think "myself."

She says to this place: I'm helping you.

There's a tap at the door.

Cowgirl goes to the table and sits where she's told, next to the only empty chair, its spot set. The three women lower their heads and hold hands, and the old woman says a prayer like it's a story about a horse. Food is passed on platters. Cowgirl eats beef and gravy and bread and vegetables, all of it heavy, condensed.

She drinks cold whole milk. Everything inside her slows. The old woman talks to the middle-aged woman about important matters, and although cowgirl recognizes the words, she can't make out what they mean, not here, and the young woman asks cowgirl kind questions, and although she understands what she's asked, she can't answer, not now, and the young woman, who notices, answers unasked questions, going into why she's enjoying college and what she does during her shifts at the gas station and where she and her boyfriend will take a drive to next weekend, and cowgirl farts. The fart is ignored.

Cowgirl says, Where are you from?

Here! laughs the young woman. I was born down the road.

Where are you *from* from? says cowgirl.

The old woman and the middle-aged woman have stopped talking.

The young woman says, How do you mean it?

Are you lost? says cowgirl.

The young woman is annoyed.

Cowgirl is annoyed. She starts to say more, but the words hitch.

The old woman nods. Go on, now.

Cowgirl stutters. She pounds the table.

Say something new! shouts the middle-aged woman. Say something we don't already get!

Cowgirl starts and stops and stops and starts.

You aren't special, says the young woman.

The young woman looks out the window.

This isn't special.

The front door bangs open. In tromps the middle-aged man from the driveway. Beside him is the young man with the face of a woman.

Cowgirl stands. She feels stuffed, sick.

The young man is dressed up and clutching flowers. His

smell nudges through the other smells, nothing like a farm or a park or a graveyard. It's insistent. He's nervous.

He tries to make his nervousness look like relief.

Cowgirl says, Come on, let's go.

They step outside. The moon is high and white and busy. They walk to the scratched-up truck.

It's not mine, says the young man. I'm borrowing it.

He opens the passenger's-side door for her.

Don't worry, when we get our own, we'll take care of it.

She doesn't move.

On the far side of the field a truck bobbles by, hauling a tall trailer of livestock. Inside the house the women put old music on. A baby cries.

That doesn't mean what you think, says the young man.

Cowgirl slips under and out of the dress.

Blushing, he urges her to get into the truck. He doesn't seem to know if he should look at her or not, but he doesn't tell her to put the dress back on.

She folds it up and gives it to him.

He tries to be okay with this.

She closes the door he opened, walks to the driver's side, and gets in. The keys curve with moonlight. She twists them. The rumble feels good as it goes through her body.

She shifts from park to neutral to drive.

The young man has dropped the flowers and the dress. He can't even cover his face. Standing there, he is a kind of question.

I'm no answer, she decides.

She coasts the driveway until it ends in the road. She takes the time to signal. Then she turns.

A Mother Buries a Gun in the Desert Again

It was loaded, I was loaded. The bottle was not the only way but it was the way that was available, my husband's way, the weakest way to make me strong. How else could I gather the fear to steal the gun from my son, to drive out of town with it in my lap, to park like a wreck on the shoulder, to stumble up a desert slope from where the city's bay of lights looked shallow?

The shovel heavy in my hands. The gun a hope in the ground. The booze hot fumes in my belly. Around me the moon dulled the bladed shapes of yucca, cacti, and shrubs. Only the strongest stars were awake and watching. The mountains looked stronger than the stars but less awake—the Sandias, the only range my family knew, watermelons returned by night to rock. What a pit to put a city in. I studied my bare arms and the tops of my breasts. My sweat prickled. My skin, my mother's, looked edible in this light. I remembered my son as a baby, in these arms and at these breasts and burping on milk I no longer made. Remembering this hurt. I made a promise to my sober self to stop remembering.

I buried the shovel next, kick-covering it in sandy dirt.

I was thirty-nine then. My son had turned sixteen. He'd tightened into a lean and stylish silence, a silence with my sister's mean blank stare, my husband's stinging smile, and my embarrassed eyes. My eyes! My eyes had been his since he opened them. The gun was a gift from a boy I hadn't met. How I saw it then was this boy had tried to steal my son. I refused to know my son's own role in stealing himself himself.

My husband saw our son's own role but this was all he saw. His refusal was to refuse knowing more than one thing at once. His way, hurried by the bottle, was hard, though no harder than mine. We discussed these ways in bed, before and after sunrise, arguments, plan-hatching, lovemaking. I was lucky then. I went to work. My husband went to work. Our son went to school.

Now I sleep on an air mattress at my sister's. My husband sleeps in his new apartment. Our son sleeps through college.

The first time I stole a gun of my son's to bury it in the desert I told my husband right when I returned. We confronted our son at breakfast. I had made my mother's chilaquiles, the meal that signaled something big, a new job, my mother's death, a move, a miscarriage. My husband put his burn-scarred fists onto the table. He told our son what I'd found. He didn't tell him how I'd buried it, how he'd wanted to take the gun to the police, to his brother, how although he'd raged at me he'd also admitted to feeling proud of me. Pride was his other way, just as hard.

Our son, looking at our faces, masked his shame in irritation and his relief in indifference. He ate.

"Where is the respect?" screamed my husband.

Our son left for school without his backpack.

"Where is it?" screamed my husband, pounding the couch.

I disagreed. "It's there, it's under things. Look for it."

"Where did he learn disrespect?"

"It's only what he's wearing."

He grabbed my arm. When I winced, the anger-strength in his grip went slack. But he held on.

"If you find another gun," he screamed, "it is mine."

I found another gun wrapped in t-shirts in a box of old toys and I drank and I drove and I buried a gun in the desert again. I was alone but everyone was with me, standing on my head. There is no other way to say it.

I pulled down my shorts by a manzanita and peed. I fell in it.

Far off, the horizontal headlights of lone cars had beginnings, middles, and endings, pushed along like golden bars. I started the car. I drove home a different way, a way I knew would meet a drunk-driving checkpoint. It was Friday.

The checkpoint gleamed at the mouth of an old mall. With its stage-like arrangement of police cars, lights, and testing stations, it had the feel of an underfunded circus. The officer who leaned into my window was not my husband's brother, but he knew our family, he'd been to our son's confirmation, he'd brought his rehabilitated wife, a card, cash. His look of gentle pity made me queasy. He was handsome.

"Take me to jail," I said.

He led me out of the car and to a bench. I watched him scratch his neck and make a phone call. Other men and women, assisted by police officers, failed walk-the-lines and breathalyzers. Some protested, some didn't. They were eased into cars and driven away like retirees. I craved retirement. A young police officer, he couldn't have been more than twenty-two, he parked my car down the block. I put my head between my knees. I threw up. I threw up again.

When I sat straight I saw that a car I knew had arrived. My husband got out of it. The police officer who'd tended to me hustled over to him. They had a disagreement. My husband, who didn't want to get back into his car, got back into his car. The police officer walked over to me.

"We know what you're doing," he said. "Don't."

My husband who was drunk drove us home.

"Where is the respect?" he said.

I disagreed but I didn't touch him. "It's there."

"Once, I can forgive. Again?"

"When it happens again we will go with your way."

My husband pounded the dashboard and made a shouting-face but didn't shout.

I made apology-orbits with my hands but didn't apologize.

He hit a median and then a curb.

At home we didn't turn on any lights. He refused to come to the bedroom. He stripped and lay on the family room couch. I stripped and lay on him. He got up and went to the bedroom, and I followed, and he got up and went to the couch, and I followed, and somewhere in the hall I hugged him, I held him where we were. We kissed.

"It isn't there," I said.

The light went on — our son had stepped out of his room.

We didn't move.

He yawned. Pajamas and sleepiness had taken half his years away.

From the end of the hall we watched him walk to the bathroom without looking our way. We watched him close the door. We listened to him lock it.

Immigrants

Our baby's first name will be ___. ___ will be born in Chicago, delivered from his mother by a doctor who will whisper in her first language while she unwinds his tangled cord. ___'s mother will be an immigrant. His father will not. Immigrants, ___ will agree, pass like coins from pockets to hands, to counters, to fields and streets and public fountains, to pockets, and if the immigrants are children when they pass the way they pass, like ___'s mother, they may find that even with four decades spent they're still between two cultures, each a currency, one worn vague but warm from being carried, the other so bright it bleaches, making things that aren't equal seem so.

___, our baby, will turn into our child.

Our child's first childcare worker's name will be Lupe. Lupe will be born in Juárez to a family that won't own their home but will own the way they are when they aren't working. Lupe will rarely not be working. Immigrants, Lupe will argue to other childcare workers, roll like tires from wherever-the-hell to here, uphill, downhill, off-hill, wobbly with the hope that the new cities they hit won't lead to leaking, to being dragged and piled and burned.

___, our child, will turn into our kid.

Our kid's first landlord's name will be Marija. Marija will be born in Zagreb, in a library, to a mother who will laugh into and out of moans and a father who will hold her, singing. Before them will stand a crowd of anxious and hopeful students.

Marija will help her tenants, also immigrants, complete their forms. Immigrants, Marija will ask her tenants, forget their favorite old-country songs because they strain to remember them, or remember their favorite old-country songs because they strain to forget them?

____, our kid, will turn into a preteen.

Our preteen's first best friend's name will be Hasan. Hasan will be born in Ramallah, on a ruined farm, to a mother and a father who will be persuaded to immigrate by mothers and fathers who were persuaded to immigrate. Hasan will study the conditions under which his parents will and will not ask him for help with their English, in grocery store lines or at the dinner table or on walks to the park, and will be unable to find a formula, the distance between their pride and their embarrassment shifting every day. Immigrants, Hasan will declare to his imam, are immigrants until they have been edged so far away from where they were born that the place in which they live becomes the place that they are closest to, but only by default.

____, our preteen, will turn into a teen.

Our teen's first favorite teacher's name will be Bea. Bea will be born in Manila to a mother who will die a day later in bed and a father who for a year will look to die on accident on the docks. Bea will wedge her classroom door open after school to start conversations in English and Spanish and Tagalog with the students who will not want to go home. Immigrants, Bea will explain to her girlfriend, are a certain order of orphan, adopted by their new country and their new-country selves, adopting ways to chat up or to shush the old-country selves that hesitate inside the limits of their new-country selves.

____, our teen, will turn into a young adult.

Our young adult's first boss's name will be Bolesław. Bolesław will be born in Buenos Aires to Warsaw refugees, to a family that will squat in one wrecked place after another. Bolesław will tell

the young adults that he will hire for his community center's summer program the stories about young adulthood that they will
think they have heard until they hear them, stories about chances,
how to grip these chances, how to lift or carry them, how to bend
or crack or free them. Immigrants, Bolesław will write to his family around the world, are between the legs of language. Legs that
kick, legs that squeeze, legs that tighten with restraint.

    ___, our young adult, will turn into a young adult who will
not know how to feel like himself.

    ___'s first love's name will be Susan. Susan will be born in
Pyongyang to respected engineers who will travel on govern-
ment business to Beijing, and from there, on family business to
Chicago, where they will move into an apartment with relatives,
change their names, and find work at a restaurant. Susan will
force the first kiss. Immigrants, Susan will think, aren't me.

    ___ will say: Immigrants are and they aren't.

    Are and aren't what? Susan will say.

    They will be riding the Red Line to a traditional Indian wed-
ding.

    ___ will be unsure of what he will mean. Embarrassed, he
will say: Americans?

    Susan will turn to the window and tap at it, saying, Do you
know what some immigrants will do to get here?

    Good things, bad things.

    To stay here?

    I've heard.

    Hearing isn't doing.

    ___ will move to hug her. It won't feel right.

    Susan will pack up for a new neighborhood and stay there, and
Bolesław will open a different community center and stay there,
and Bea will ignore the pressure to retire early and stay there, and
Hasan will attend college in New York City and stay there, and

Marija will fly home to care for her aging family and stay there, and Lupe will be promoted to administration and stay there.

___ will look at world maps in bed. He will be seesawed by a homesickness for the places he will not be born into knowing. He will feel, again, like a somebody else.

He will trudge downstairs and say to us, How can I be expected to stay?

We will pour him tea or coffee or homemade liqueur. We will say that this is the kind of question that one can grow up around.

___ will travel to Hong Kong to meet his mother's people, and he will travel to Lagos and Abuja to meet his father's parents' people, and he will return to Chicago, feeling, he will say, that he has learned just enough about the what and the how of where his people come from to seal him off from them more completely.

He will trudge in through the front door and sit at our table to think.

We will serve him the food that he will have missed the most. We will say that these are the kinds of questions that one can live through, or around, or on top of.

Or under, we will admit.

___ will say: I can wait to find out. But then I will go.

We will watch him eat what we have made. We will hope: that he can wait, that he can go. That when he wants to, he can come back.

Small Boy

The small boy says to his big sister, "Why did we kill all the Indians?"

They're in the basement playing a video game. Both of them are white.

"We didn't kill them," says his big sister, "our ancestors did."

"Why did our ancestors kill all the Indians?"

"Okay, not really *our* ancestors because Dad's family came in the twenties and Mom's in the sixties and the Indians were already totally dead by then, mostly."

"Why did ancestors kill all the Indians?"

"But I guess you could say it *was* us, pretty much, because today we're basically the same culture as the culture of the people who killed the Indians back then. And it's 'Native Americans,' not 'Indians.' 'Indians' is ignorant."

The small boy says to his angry stepmom, "Why did we kill all the Native Americans?"

They're returning from the grocery store in hardly any traffic. Plastic bags stuffed with food rustle in the backseat.

"We didn't kill all of them," says his angry stepmom. "The ones that are still around have problems and are in poverty. Like the minorities."

"Why did we kill most of the Native Americans?" says the small boy to his principal. His principal is black. They're at recess on the playground. Other small boys and girls of many colors shout and run, arguing the rules of the games they make up.

"We didn't just kill them," says his principal, taking off her glasses to rub her eyebrows, which she does when she's about to say something she expects her students to remember, "we erased them. We erased their histories and traditions and languages, their cultures. Did you know that there are tribes not around anymore that we don't even know one thing about? We know more about some dinosaurs than we do about some tribes."

"Why did we erase most of the Native Americans?" says the small boy to the tall girl he likes. The tall girl he likes is white. They're at a birthday party in the park. Both have bright balloons tied to their wrists.

"We didn't," says the tall girl he likes, "they did it to themselves by not being advanced enough in their civilization, if they were advanced enough in their civilization they wouldn't have been erased."

The small boy tugs at his balloon-string. He doesn't want to disagree with the tall girl he likes, but he feels disagreement sticking together inside him. It's heavy. He thinks he might be sick. He says, "If they were more advanced in their civilization, would they have erased us?"

The tall girl bops him on the top of the head with her balloon.

He waves his hands to defend himself. "What if it was a tie, would we have erased each other?"

The tall girl bops him in the face with her balloon. It hurts his nose. Smirking, she skips away to join a group of other tall girls who are laughing at a group of other small boys. The small boys squeeze each other's balloons, trying to get as close as possible to popping them without actually popping them.

"We wouldn't," says the small boy to his big gray dog.

They're sitting in weedy grass in the backyard. It's quiet in the dark apartment building, over the rotten fences, and in the alley where the small boy is not supposed to go. He still feels sick. Disagreement hardens inside him.

The big gray dog chews on a broken branch. Knots clunk across its teeth.

The small boy touches the big gray dog's chest like he's taking an oath. He again pretends that the big gray dog's every action contains a hidden message, one he can catch if he focuses hard or loosens up. He focuses hard. He loosens up. Before he can say for sure what he has or hasn't caught, he falls asleep.

Driving in the Early Dark, Ted Falls Asleep

Ted drives.

Ted tells himself, Ted drives.

Ted tells himself, Too tired to sleep too tired to sleep too tired to.

Ted chokes the wheel and slaps the wheel, hissing, "Don't! you! forget! this!" His words become hot breath — his hot breath, fingers — the fingers wend into his eyes.

The sun is cracking, struggling behind a headboard of clouds. The sky not brightening so much as leaking night, the only thing worth watching no matter how much they move. No matter how much they move, Oklahoma doesn't. It is fucking everywhere.

Ted thinks, How about some heat? He clicks the knob: ON.

Some heat presses like a pillow into Ted's unwashed face, his nose, the skinny brushes of his eyebrows.

Some heat nods Ted's head toward the wheel he's slapped and choked.

Ted jolts — he clicks the knob: OFF. The chill returns, banking back like a fog. To his right, Constance sleeps, a Navajo blanket laying skirt-like on her lap. Her face tucked away to the window. In the backseat, their boxes. In their boxes, their things. They are moving, them and their things, for her Chicago job. Celebrate. Say goodbye to Arizona and all their Arizona friends and all their Arizona miseries. Hit the road and drive all day to the bar at the Best Western in Oklahoma City, to two pitchers and stuffed potato skins and taking turns trying not to fall asleep, not to look at anything, any who are we, any what now.

The tab to her credit card. Practice. They weren't old but they might be.

And now they're moving in the early dark of their last day on the road and could die if Ted falls asleep but Ted's too tired to fall asleep, "So don't!" he whispers, "Don't forget!" and he grinds his gummy eyes—thumb in one, index in the other, a truck across the turnpike rolling glare along the windshield, painting his hands white.

Think! Talk! Ted!

Thinking talking Ted, to wake, recalls famous times he's fallen asleep.

Last night: back from the hotel bar, Constance gave out a shuddering sigh and shook her body and looked him down, and despite their lack of whatever it was, wanted to, right then. They peeled off their sitting-sweaty clothes and slammed together on sheets that stank of cleaning agents.

Sex began.

"You're drooling."

"No way," he said, waking, wiping his chin, "where?" She squirmed off and over, rubbing her face in fury.

Buckets of white glare—two trucks across the turnpike, side by side, one in passing. Ted runs his fingers on the ribbing of the wheel. Constance shifts and twists her blanket. Ted blinks with force: his right eye flutters.

The eyelid spasms. Is spasming.

With each convulsion it feels less and less like flesh, more and more like someone else's curtain. When it stops jerking, it mashes shut.

Ted's brother Big Michael used to mash butterflies. Touch this, Ted, it's sticky.

It'll turn you on, Ted.

Big Michael moved to Houston to sell homes.

"They trust him with their futures!" says Ted.

Big Michael married Hadiza, the laser scientist.

"Her too!" says Ted.

"Wake up!" says Ted.

Ted attempts to blink his eye open. He needs it working by Chicago to look for jobs, to look for marriage to Constance. He scrunches his cheek and massages the lid. Stars spark behind the heavy blackness, winking into the vision of his other eye, but the lid stays sealed.

Ted tries to click the closed eye to ON. ON, he clicks, ON.

The eye stays OFF.

Ted turns up the music. One man whistling. Ted tries to whistle with him.

Ted punches off the music. It flickers back on, weakly, then peters out, going until gone. Constance and her Navajo skirt are also gone, blanketed to Ted's right by the blackness of his jammed lid.

Ted remembers falling asleep on her lap.

Ted remembers falling asleep while she was falling asleep on his lap.

Ted remembers when he used to feel happy waking her to talk.

"Because we'll be together, Ted," says Ted, mimicking Constance.

"We've come together, Michael," says Ted, mimicking Hadiza.

Everyone meeting everyone at the majestic wedding.

What do you do?

We're moving.

Thinking about marriage?

We're moving.

The last dance. Hadiza, the lady of lasers, hugging Big Michael's arm, astonished. Big Michael, the masher of butterflies, patting Hadiza's butt, astonished.

Constance dancing Ted off the dance floor, saying, "When will we love each other like that?"

When we're together forever.

That's what I'm asking!

They kiss. The kiss is bad.

Ted touches his closed eye. He tries to remember people he used to know, the ones he liked, and that's when the middle-aged man he used to work with, the gray-bearded bastard who slept with one eye open, grumbles from the boxes in the back.

The best summer job that Ted has ever had: Public Works, high school.

"Best *job* job," Ted says, yawning, driving trucks, chipping trees, watering Hadizas, staying awake. Awake. Burt. Bart?

"Burke," croaks Ted, blinking with his open eye, clutching a rake in his first week with old man Burke at the noisy helm of a backhoe digging a pit in a park, sweating, the engine howling, Ted watching that dirty yellow bucket scoop and move, scoop and move, like chewing holes in the earth was the only work worth doing—until the bucket froze, mid-air.

Ted hustled over to peek into the cab. Burke, buffeted by the growl of the machine, asleep at the controls. One of his eyes open. Heavy-lidded and drowsy and drugged, but open. Ted crept closer.

"Burke!" he shouted.

The man awoke, his open eye unglazing.

"Look, kid. I'm older than you'll be when you're my age."

What we have, we're losing?

"Lemme put it this way. How much you hate love."

I'm moving.

"Not enough, you aren't."

Burke sinks into the dance floor, banging the bucket and shouting, "No new job's gonna do it!"

The breakroom. Burke's one-eyed catnaps after his meatball sandwich, the shaded windows leaking night. Burke tips back in his chair, hands folded on his Oklahoma, and dozes, wheezing, whistling, one lid jammed open—the eyeball unstatic, it floats and flickers, petering.

Eli—the only other summer kid, the trickster who joined the army at the end of June—who made work not work with jokes—their imitations of everyone, of each other—their pranks on Burke—where will you go on your tour, when will you come back from your tour—we'll email—don't forget him—Ted forgot him—together they approach the strangeness of sleeping Burke, Eli waving a permanent marker.

"Let's draw a dick," he whispers, dead or wounded.

"With hearts for balls," whispers Ted, attending college.

"This won't work," says Constance, relieved. She tugs up her turnpike: between her legs, her naked back.

Eli pops the marker's cap. Big Michael smears sold homes. They lean in, smell a car crash, and see their smoking breath.

Burke, one eye drooling, in a voice choked by wheels of sleep, says, "Don't ask."

When you sleep with one eye open, what do you see with the eye that's open?

Burke takes a bite of the road.

Eli says, "I'm going to die."

Ted is crying. "Don't."

Eli dies. Burke dies. Constance dies. Big Michael lives with Hadiza.

Ted dies and wakes to Oklahoma everywhere, the white line waving, headlights hauling blinding paint. The board of night explodes.

I want to live awake?
Ted clicks his open eye to ON.
ON, he clicks.
ON.
ON.

Drunk in Texas, Two New Friends Talked Horses

Drunk in Texas, two new friends talked horses. They slouched at an icehouse picnic table in the sweaty black lap of an evening fat with heat. One had ridden twice, the other never.

"Majestic," they agreed, again, and imagined horses running and rearing and leaping, majestically.

It was when they hit "How come?" that they for the first time disagreed. This friendly friction whipped them back to lively states: their heads broke the surface of the heat.

The one who'd ridden twice — tall and trim-bearded, from Illinois, in this Texas town to teach at its university — tapped with his empty bottle the bench-seat he straddled and put forth that the majesty of the horse, for man and woman alike, could be found in the fact of putting so much other-minded muscle between one's legs.

"And moving it," he said, flapping an imaginary hat. "Or with it. Through it."

The other, who'd ridden never — strong and bald, from Pennsylvania, in this Texas town to coordinate information technologies at its university's library — stood up to sit on the table's blistered top, his feet at his new friend's hip. From there he saw the bobbing heads of other patrons, bros and bright-flanneled hipsters, their bodies bent in conversation, the lot of them looking like one extended family. His aunt, who'd died the day he'd left for Texas, had bought, sold, and shown horses. She'd often boasted that when checking "woman" on state forms, she'd add the prefix "horse-" in crunchy cursive. Remembering her many maxims, the man from Pennsylvania ventured to disagree with his new friend from Illinois, arguing that the horse's majesty lay not in muscle or movement—though the roles these features played were often mistaken for the starring ones—but in the animal's hardnosed sensitivity, which greenhorns took for irritability, laziness, or brainlessness, which any rider worth their tack recognized for what it properly was: an emotional intelligence that, when addressed in kind, split the hardest hearts with springs of fondness.

"Horses are dumb as hell at being people," he concluded. "But they're goddamn smart at being horses."

Two tables down, a woman stood. She looked complete in every way.

She slung her heavy purse.

She grinned at something said.

Her laugh opened, an earthy low—a rich brown river in a rich green valley.

The two new friends had spoken to her earlier. Both had forgotten her name, but remembered it as musical; both had imagined the warmth of waking with her daily; one had imagined the warmth of waking with her lasting until ending, through what passed for good fortune, in old age, illness, and death. Before they'd talked horses they'd talked women, the women who hadn't moved with them to Texas. Then the reasons why, and the reasons for those reasons, and whether reasons were women, or women reasons, and before long their talk had ranged so far and wide that where they settled was the future they wished upon one another.

The woman left.

The man from Illinois tooted a note on his empty bottle's mouth. He brushed the bottle-mouth against his beard, circling his own mouth, and listened to the scritching of his facial hair.

For the first time in months he felt close to something fundamental. Since the move, every fundamental something had been too far away to touch. Why had he taken this job? Why had he left the women he'd left? Why was he closer to forty than to thirty?

Why was he always who he was, even when he wasn't?

With the help of his new friend from Pennsylvania, he hoped he might creep near enough. "What you say may be true," he said, pressing the issue, "but there's only one way to know a horse, and it's through the gateway of your loins."

The man from Pennsylvania rolled his beer can across his bare head, a worthless attempt at relief from the heat. He said, "Too simple to be true," and told the story his aunt had told last Thanksgiving, when she'd been spry and well, when they'd lived where gray light and hard wind had made of any trip outside a brisk and bitter drink. Someone she'd called a "lonely lawyer woman" had shareboarded one of her old horses. She'd taken lessons and was an okay rider, though too timid to be truly skilled. On the nights she came to the barn she'd walk the horse into the round pen, circle once or twice, then lead him out and to a bench, where she sat. From her purse she'd pull a bottle of wine. With one hand loose on the rope she'd describe her divorce, getting louder though not meaner as she drank. She'd bring the horse's head to hers and nuzzle.

His aunt knew this, having once stayed back to watch from behind a bush.

On mornings after the lonely lawyer-woman's visits, the old horse's muzzle would be pocked with lipstick in little skipping prints.

"Another gateway altogether," said the man from Pennsylvania.

The man from Illinois had listened closely. He flicked a crumb from his beard and said, "That's invasive."

This irritated the man from Pennsylvania, though he wasn't

sure who or what his new friend had called invasive. His irrita-tion, because it felt unfounded, slumped into shame — his shame moped to another memory: years ago, his aunt, who'd kept keys to his parents' house, had moseyed through the front door to find him on the family room couch, whacking off.

"Wish I could tell you how to do it right," she'd said with a laugh.

"Muscle and movement," chanted the man from Illinois, waving his hand like a hypnotist, no longer addressing the man from Pennsylvania, "the movement of muscles, muscled move-ment, majesty," and these words broke loose a jammed-up mem-ory he'd been unknowingly tugging at since their talk had turned to horses, the memory, he now knew, that had supplied his argu-ment. With his hands on something solid at last, he whooped, fix-ing to ride it as hard as he could.

He scrambled to the top of the table. He clap-clap-clapped. He stomped.

He kicked an ashtray — it exploded on the pavement — and with gusto spilled his story to the icehouse patio: sixth grade out-door education! A weekend trip to Southern Illinois! A goddamn dumpy ranch! They'd milked dumb cows and charted dumb stars and on the last day, they rode the fucking horses. He'd been ter-rified to be away from home and on a horse, then bored as they tromped single-file through the ranch's meager acres, then mes-merized as he watched the horse in front of him start shitting, its anus like the inside of a mouth, a chewing in reverse, and finally, awestruck as the ride ended at the stables, where their social stud-ies teacher, a chaperone, mounted a spotted mare like he'd been doing it every morning of his life. This teacher was a squat and expressive man, respected only by dorks, mocked for missing one and a half of his fingers, the pathetic result of an accident in his father's Chicago sausage shop where he'd worked for candy bars. Atop the horse, however, he was an altogether different entity. He kicked into a canter, a gallop, a wild but measured blasting back-and-forth that opened the mouths of all the girls and boys who watched. He'd even yeehawed.

"A horse," shouted the man from Illinois, "complete in itself, incompleted by the rider it completes. But incompletely."

Many had left their tables. Those who remained stared or pretended not to, in fear or in reverence.

The man from Illinois lowered his voice, as if about to remove his clothes. "The second time I rode I thought too much and fell off," he said. He clinked his smile with his bottle. "Two broken teeth."

"Ow," he said, touching his face.

The man from Pennsylvania, meanwhile, had stood up and stepped back to better watch his new friend's storytelling. Through it, his own shame and irritation had been carried off, though a grainy jealousy remained. That he felt this seemed uncharitable. Still more uncharitable was the feeling that followed: he knew he would leave the icehouse and his new friend, right now, without a word, not unlike how he'd left Pennsylvania and his dying aunt, how Pennsylvania and his dead aunt had left him. He was in touch with being out of touch, he thought, again. He ended his beer in one gulp and tossed it at the garbage bin. The can airballed badly. A grim barback built like a retired boxer stooped to pick it up. He lurked closer. The man from Pennsylvania stumbled away, his head shining with sweat.

"I used to want to ride them," said the man from Illinois, wobbling. "Now I only want to break one."

"If you do," said a woman he couldn't see, "hold on to the mane. It's the head that kills you."

"The head!" he screamed, and he lobbed his bottle over the icehouse and into the street, where, out of sight, it shattered.

Snake Canyon

B. and Y. took the road without a name to Snake Canyon. Again they looked for signs. None.

"Snake Canyon Road?" said B.

He braked over a bump. The old car bobbed and rocked. They passed another high desert subdivision, a half-completed housing development ribbed with the skeletons of homes that would have big-windowed views of the valley. No one was at work on them this afternoon. The only signs read, FOR SALE.

Y. waved. "Maybe the road's between names."

"It has an old name," said B. "I want to know it."

Y. made his tell-a-joke face. "Bill Bigley?"

"Bill Bigley" was the possibly fake name of a man whose mail had been coming for months to B.'s apartment — oversized envelopes, beat-up packages from out of state, RESPONSE RE-QUIRED notices from local agencies — all of which B. handed back to friendly but indifferent mail carriers. "Bill Bigley" had become what B. and Y. said instead of saying, What the hell can you do? or Good luck, jackass. Lately it'd begun to mean, Let's get a goddamn beer. Many goddamn beers had been got — B. and Y. had hit the last week of their first year of graduate school, the both of them history students, hardworking would-be scholars from places other than the southwest.

Snake Canyon, the canyon they hiked once a month, hunched low in a high range. The car took the steep bend toward it, jud-dering — the development vanished; on one side, the rise of sheer

rock and broken ridges, and on the other, the open desert bris-
tling in heat and haze all the way to the horizon. They talked
of final projects. Fat bugs spattered the windshield. They passed
smashed animals, the buzzards that slow-flapped into flight away
from the bodies, and the entrance to a private drive, its black gate
shut. The nameless road ended in a nameless gravel causeway,
which kicked on for a mile until curling into a little empty lot.
They parked.

They slammed doors and stepped into the living stillness.

The air was clean and dry, but flush with the feeling they'd
come for: an emptying out: an emptying in. A reminder that they
were made out of their bodies.

B. slapped on sunscreen. Y. one-shouldered his backpack.

They hiked the trail through a scrappy landscape scrubbed
brown and red, green and yellow-golden. Far-off peaks and slopes
stood, sat, or stretched in great basins of sun and shadow. Within
reach were feather-tipped grasses, clusters of thriving cacti, lonesome stands of trees. Dark beetles zipped and clicked.

Y. stopped near a skinny gulch. "Smell that?"

B. made a show of sniffing.

Y. said, "Musky, musky-fresh. Alive!"

"Smells like beard," said B., grinning through his. He fin-
ger-twisted a knotty tuft. The director of their program joked
weekly that B.'s beard grew B., not the other way around. Its
thickness made him look more rustic than he was. He enjoyed
his comforts, he liked to say. A big man.

With his foot Y. tapped a clot of dirt into the gulch. He was
clean-shaven and short-haired, as thin as a teenager. He fixed a
stare on anyone he listened to, often through their pauses, which
made him seem judgmental. Special reserves of funding had re-
cruited him. He wore a chewed-up straw hat he'd bought abroad.

A sheet of shadow crossed the canyon like the turning of a
page.

The little mountain appeared, the one they knew. They'd gone off-trail to scale it every time they'd come. It was of a climbable incline, dotted in dead trees and wiry bushes, and at its peak it wore a shallow slab-like cave. A black tongue of shade extended from the cleft. When the trail got as close as it would to the base, B. and Y. broke off into the pathless high desert. They trudged through grasses. Every step scattered scores of insects. The little mountain, modest from a distance, swelled skyward as they approached.

"Let's name this mountain," said B.

Y. stroked his chin in an exaggerated way. "Let's name this mountain—let's name this mountain Let's Name This Mountain Mountain."

"Original. Accurate."

"It's probably close! To the 'old name'. . ."

Behind a heap of prickly pear opened a clear draw onto the base. They jogged up it in one go and began to crouch-climb, pathfinding. One part calculation, one part intuition. Secure sure footing. Maintain momentum. Skirt the likely lairs of deadly animals. They'd never seen a mountain lion, they'd never seen a snake. Scorpions, tarantulas, yes. Loose rocks chuckled when they misstepped. As their eyes went down, easy spaces entered their conversation, changing its shape. They traded monologues. Their hearts thudded, their legs fired. No shade until the top.

Embarrassing, argued B., that neither of them knew Snake Canyon's history. What indigenous peoples, what settlers, how it had been named. Embarrassing not just because they studied history, but because here they were, contributing to the larger problem: Americans not knowing the history of American places. A problem that could be remedied, and when remedied, could remedy even larger American problems.

Y. agreed. He added that this problem's source could be found in the short-term advantages to overlooking history. By intentionally or unintentionally overlooking history, American communities could choose to shape and be shaped by imagined futures that, at least initially, appeared untouched by American mistakes, by American embarrassments. Freedom in forgetting.

"Look at the way that cities grow out here," he said. "They get big without knowing where they've come from."

"They ignore where they are."

"Continually."

"They can only see themselves from the inside out."

Beneath them the surface changed: steeper, with bigger rocks. The light felt heavy on their backs.

"We need more embarrassment," said B. He sopped his face with his shirt.

Y. said, "We could start by seeing that it's already here."

"It's not enough to look."

Y. took off his hat to scratch his head. He stared at B. "Fact."

Brown birds darted above them, moving so fast their folded bodies hissed.

They sprinted the last stretch to make the cave's shade. Then they were in its mouth. A deep coolness settled onto their limbs. They sat on cold stone.

Y. opened his backpack.

"Cave Mountain," announced B., patting the ground. He thumbed at the cave walls. "Cave Mountain Cave."

They cracked tallboys. Y. made three toasts: one to Cave Mountain Cave on Cave Mountain, one to how the act of giving old places new names obliterated the desire to discover old places' "old names," and one to B.'s lack of consistency. B. toasted to Y.'s ability to confuse a man's jokes for a man's serious scholarly interests. Y. toasted to B.'s inability to admit that the two were the same. B. toasted to being a dick. Y. toasted to the dickiest dick they didn't know, Bill Bigley.

They laughed and drank and called each other names.

They ate peanuts and trail mix.

They talked about their girlfriends, about long-distance dating and in-program dating.

Y. said, "You pretend to be the people you've always been. You aren't. You're always changing a little—in this case, changing a little in separate places, changing in response to those separate places. If you live in the same place you don't notice the little changes, but if you live apart, when you finally get to see each other again, you notice, and the little changes feel big. You feel cheated. You pretend not to notice and you pretend not to feel cheated. You pretend you're who you were."

"What are some of your little changes? I can't imagine you changing."

"I'll tell you when I see her next week."

They opened two more tallboys.

"Class, guest lectures, bars, parties," said B., "you're with each other everywhere, all the fucking time. You start to think you've seen every side of each other. You get really sure. Because of that you dig ditches, ditches you pack each other into. Don't step out of that ditch! Every relationship gets there, it's just that when you date in the program it gets there fast."

"Little changes, ditches . . . definitions . . ."

"Definitions," agreed B. "But it's mostly good to be defined."

"The little changes, those are what push you outside. Outside of the definitions."

"Or into the definitions."

"'The difference is merely qualitative,'" declared Y., imitating a professor they didn't like, a man out of touch with every class he taught.

They kicked around inside the shallow cave.

They threw rocks, flat ones that exploded down the mountain.

They discussed other students in the program, the ones who'd grab up the fellowships, grants, and jobs. They outlined what they themselves intended to do with their degrees. Since last semester they'd changed their minds more than once, right there on the mountain. They wondered: How else would they change their minds, and what would be the whys? Years from now, what would they make of their years here? How would they argue that what had happened here had led to who they would be by then becoming?

They stepped to far ends of the same bush and pissed.

"I've been thinking," said Y. "It's important to have fame."

"You're in the wrong field," said B., and thought: But you will. Everyone bends the fuck over backwards for you.

"Oh, I know. I mean in-our-field fame. One book, one article that's cited for decades. Like with Dr. Z. Not because I want everyone to know me, but because it will make me make my work better."

B. said he didn't agree but he knew what he meant.

"It's not personal," said Y., looking at B. and thinking: You will never make it.

They crushed the cans and stuffed them into the backpack.

You won't have to work as hard, thought one.

You're not willing to work it every way, thought the other.

Both thought, The work.

That's it, that's all, that's everything.

"Ready?" they said.

They high- and low-fived.

They ran down the mountain. The grade pulled them fast, then faster. Legs loose, eyes quick, they rode their own momentum into elevated states of action, an unthinking done to them by their bodies, a sensation within and without at once as they covered ground, skip-sliding, pivoting to dodge cholla and yucca and barrel cacti, tapping tree trunks for balance, stomping to slow down and leaping to speed up and laying out a long and crunching track of noise and dust until Y. fell, with a shout.

B. staggered to a stop, nearly going down himself. From where he wound up he couldn't make out Y., only where the bank of dust ended.

"You all right?" he yelled.

A dry rattle, loud and rising.

B. picked up a heavy stone and hustled over.

The rattle ceased.

Sitting up, Y. was separating himself from the gnarled gray branches of the ocotillo he'd landed in. Its curved thorns scritched out of his shirt. He was hatless, without his backpack, his arms bleeding. After B. helped him to his feet, Y. unbuttoned his jeans, tugging them past his boxers to just above his knee. Two marks glistened high on his thigh. They drooled blood.

"I stepped on a snake, I fell, the snake bit me," said Y., making his tell-a-joke face. "Through my jeans."

B. checked his phone. No signal this far inside the canyon, but there'd be a low one closer to the lot. What muscle there was on Y.'s thigh was already darkening, inflating. B. knew enough about snakebites to know that with immediate medical attention everything would be okay. Y. had read that too, somewhere, but had the feeling it would have been better if the snake had bitten him lower.

Both stared at the snakebite as if it would speak.

B. had been speaking, saying things since checking his phone. He looked away from the wound and stopped. He couldn't remember a word of what he'd said.

Y. pulled up his pants. When he buttoned them he felt as if he had stood up inside himself.

—inside himself and at the bottom of himself.

The bottom of himself was a narrow black ravine. The narrow black ravine ran into and out of a crooked darkness. The self that had stood up inside himself touched the walls of the narrow black ravine. This caused crazy echoes.

Everything the standing self did caused crazy echoes: breathing, blinking, feeling.

"How are you feeling?" said B.

They were easing down the mountainside as fast as they could, B. staying close. Because of the grade they walked in zigzags.

Y. answered, "Not enough on the outside, too much on the inside."

B. backed up. He rerouted them around a dip.

"It means I feel like I was bitten by a rattlesnake," said Y.

"That's all right: you were."

"It bit me, it rattled, it left."

B.'s hands hovered at Y.'s side as he hobbled around a many-bladed agave.

The mountainside became less steep. Some distance away, the legs of the trail wobbled in the heat. Beyond that sat the valley's city-haze, foul and lazy.

Everything B. said began with his saying they'd be in the lot before they knew it.

"It rattled after," said Y. "Afterthought."

B. said that that was all right.

"All right!" said Y., make-a-joking.

At a juniper Y. winced. He bent as if he would puke.

B. put their arms around each other. Together they straggled, their legs working like stilts. Their balance wavered. "Hold it," said B., adjusting their limbs, and when he noticed that Y.'s arm, streaked and sticky with blood from the fall, had streaked his own arm sticky, he felt as if he had walked out on himself.

— walked out on himself and turned back to watch.

The self that had walked out crossed its arms. It was proud of the self it had walked out on. The self it had walked out on was moving a friend calmly through the muddy cloud of a crisis. Every move that self made made the watching self shudder with pride.

Y. puked, a thin and beery froth. It sprayed both their shoes.

"Almost to the trail," said B., keeping them moving, "almost to the lot."

Y. started to say something but stopped himself.

B. pretended not to notice.

Y. spat.

B.'s watching self sighed, proud of the puke on the shoes of the self it had walked out on.

Y.'s at-the-bottom-of-himself self listened to the sound of the puking crazy-echo into howls.

B.'s watching self practiced the story the self it had walked out on would tell for years to amazed others, the story of what was being watched: a rescue.

Y.'s at-the-bottom-of-himself self crouched. It listened between the echoes for the beating of its heart. Instead it heard the echoes.

It sat down: echoes.

It curled up: echoes.

They hurried, sweating and panting. Their talk had dried up.

Near the base of the little mountain they tripped on tree roots and fell.

B. rushed to his feet. His shorts snagged on a yucca and change tinkled from his pockets. Y. lay sprawled on his back, very still, his eyes fearsome. Creases of pain folded his face. Where he'd cut his arms was pink with dust. B. leaned so that his shadow shaded Y.

Y. turned his awful stare to B.

B. wanted to look away but didn't.

Y. held his breath for what seemed to be too long, as if strangling it. He inhaled with a gasp.

B. shivered, spooked. For a moment he was the self that had walked out and the self that had been walked out on, all at once. He felt a tightening of guilt and panic. His body ached.

Y. shivered too. For a moment he was only at the bottom of himself.

Neither was where they were as they looked at each other.

"Up," said B., reaching out.

They left the little mountain's base for flat land. They pushed on through the grasses toward the trail. The distances they knew had lengthened, widened, thickened. Y.'s mouth smacked dry. He talked about pain, his voice caked and pasty.

"As if it's just in your head! As if *you're* just in your head. You're also in your thigh," he said, pointing. "You're in your blood, you're in your blood on somebody else, your puke on somebody else. Your sweat."

"Fact," said B.

"I should have pissed on you too."

B. agreed.

"I should have pissed on you when I had the chance."

"Yes," said B.

Y.'s face was as pale as B.'s was red. He licked his teeth. "How about a drink."

The bottled water was in the backpack they'd left behind. B. said, "I'm pretty sure there's extra in the trunk."

Y. said, "Fact."

They reached the trail, the familiar view from its bend, the familiar crunch of its gravelly stones. B. tried to punch through to 911. "Almost there."

Y. broke from B. and yelled in pain. He thrashed his arms about.

B. held out his hands but didn't touch Y.

Y. unbuttoned. He jerked down his jeans, and by accident, his boxers. His thigh and hip and abdomen were bloated, mottled dark with ugly swelling. Purple-green rashes crosshatched the bite marks. Looking at them, he felt high and whole with fury, with a wanting to go back to before he'd been bitten and a wanting to stop wanting to go back. There was no before to go back to. The snake was a dusty blink, a dark lashing and unlashing. He wanted to stop and he wanted to go, he couldn't go, he couldn't stop.

"You know?" he said, though he hadn't said any of this out loud.

B. nodded, staying where he was, hands out. He wanted to say and do the right thing, and at the same time, to say and do nothing. He wanted to be stronger than he was.

Y. tried to tug his boxers and jeans back up but couldn't without clenching his teeth and fighting a scream.

"Wait," said B., moving forward. He helped Y. to pull his boxers and jeans all the way off—the flash of Y.'s white skin and black hair and penis, half-erect—and he wrapped the jeans around Y.'s waist. He tied the legs together. He squatted and said, "Get on."

They lumbered down the trail, Y. piggybacking on B.

Y.'s arms around B.'s neck made the both of them run with sweat. Their steps were firm and thoughtless.

B. asked Y. a question.

Y. answered, "When?"

B. tried to answer this answer but had forgotten the question he'd just asked. His face and beard dripped. His legs quivered. In him rose a jagged annoyance. He felt a bit like he was being studied, like his actions would be used against him by know-nothings he'd never meet. The annoyance sharpened into anger. In his ear Y. began to breathe strangely, poppingly.

B. asked him another question.

Y. said something that sounded like, "Who."

"What?" said B.

Y. said something that sounded like, "Who-ohw."

Y. said it again.

Y. said, "Ohw-how."

B. dropped to a knee and sat Y. on the trail. He held him up. A more pale paleness was pooling in Y.'s face.

Terrified, B. fireman-lifted Y.: he helped him to his feet from behind, crouched in front of him, and raised him onto his shoulders. He'd learned this lift in a high school summer camp he'd hated, where his helpless partner, his size, had dropped him on his head. B. gripped Y.'s arms with one arm and Y.'s legs with the other. His spine flared. He hustled down the trail—he shouted things and forgot them, all of them, and shout-sang a running cadence he'd learned at the same hated summer camp, a lewd one, and searing hands of pain made fists inside his body but he didn't feel his body, not truly, and in this contradiction he came into the presence of some still greater pain, a trembling too big to be known in any one present, and on his shoulders Y. went twice as heavy.

Twice as heavy was the only way he'd ever say it.

B. set Y. down. The jeans had fallen off. B. checked Y.'s wrists for a pulse and his mouth for a breath, but his own hard breathing was in the way and he checked without looking Y. in the face. He fireman-lifted Y. Shit smeared from Y. onto B.'s shorts and shirt.

In the lot he lay Y. out on the hood of the car. Y.'s bare legs squeaked against the metal. B. leaned on the hood to rest, to catch his breath, but jumped back—the hot surface burned his hands. He looked at Y., who hadn't moved. He lifted him off the hood and rolled him into the backseat, facedown. The black wound oozed.

He took a bottle of water from the trunk and drank it, shaking. At this moment the too-big trembling was the only thing he felt. Later, out of the canyon, he would try to understand this feeling. There were Y.'s parents and siblings and nieces, and Y.'s girlfriend, and Y.'s other friends, and B. There were the times that they would never have, all of them, yes. What was worse, though, what really fed the feeling, were the times that they would have never had no matter what, even if, the times they had misled one another into imagining as sure. These were the times B. hoped he could forget. It would take work.

He started the car. He drove down the nameless causeway and the nameless road. The second his phone flickered a signal he pulled over, just before the entrance to the half-finished subdivision. This close he could see the rows of partly built houses, the piles of bricks, boards, and stones, the dirt roads that would be paved. The call went through.

POST-WEST

Big Lonesome Endings

THE TRAIN TO PENNSYLVANIA

The cowboy boarded the train to Pennsylvania. He pushed into an empty compartment, took a window-seat, and bunched his bag behind his head. In it were the clothes he couldn't sell.

For three days sleep sat and stood inside his body.

He reached for what he could remember of Pennsylvania, where he'd come from years ago, and then for what he would remember of the southwest, where he'd come from now. The reaching led to aching. Mostly he watched the land through the window.

The land tripped through splintered desert-mountains.

The land fell flat against the fertile boards of Illinois, Indiana, Ohio.

The land tumbled across green hills and into valleys, the pur-pled rock of low piney mountains, the rivers long and wealthy, Pennsylvania.

At times men in suits of a sort the cowboy had never seen would clunk open the door to his compartment, take one step in, then one step out. After they'd left, the cowboy would touch his face: still swollen.

In him, sleep itself began to reach and ache.

On the ride's last evening he squinted at a puddle of a sunset. He'd told the woman who'd touched him last that Pennsylvania was where he'd come from way back when. This no longer felt true. Pennsylvania was where he'd been coming from at all times, wherever he was, even here, in it again.

Whenever he woke it was with his face against the window.

PENNSYLVANIA

The station had been renovated and neglected, built up and let go. On its sooty ceiling pilgrims and tribesmen traded without touching. The cowboy followed two old men across the cracked marble floor and to the exit. He sniffed himself as he went. He stank.

His hometown and homestate opened all around him all at once—the smell of mud and spring, the hustling squat-limbed loggers, the square women with scarred hands, the packs of frowning children playing games he knew. Sorry horses drank from troughs. Trucks loaded with tree limbs guttered by. Every breeze brought pollen, woodsmoke, sawdust. The cowboy took off his hat. What he saw here wasn't the same, it was true, but it wasn't different either, and these opposing facts, horn-locked, kicked up the choking cloud he found himself inside. On that street his mother had slipped in sideways rain. At that corner his sister had given a man who'd loved her a piecrust packed with horseshit. In that alley his older brother had tried to open his own throat with a broken bottle. In this saloon his father had tapped the cowboy's chin with his bad hand and said, "What all's here?"

"All's yonder now," his father had answered, speaking through his son to his younger self, offering his younger self too-late never-woulds and never-weres, no more maybes, somedays, somehows. The cowboy had seen then that this was how the man had always been. It had made him want to leave more than everything else. Their barkeep set out another shot, another beer, the evening on the house. They drank that evening down.

The cowboy sat on the curb outside this saloon that was saloon no more. A tidy tailor shop. Through the warped window a young man dressed like an old man wiped a magnifying glass and sneezed. The cowboy touched his face—he'd forgotten his bag on the train.

"Poet," said a longhaired man.

The longhaired man stood behind the cowboy, close enough to touch him with a cane he didn't have. Not old, he was aged, his folded face as stained as the suit he wore, as once-fine, a suit of the sort the cowboy knew.

The longhaired man tipped his hat, which matched. He said, "Words in you."

From the curb the cowboy stared back, hoping to give the impression of holding his ground. He didn't know if he should know this man.

The longhaired man opened and closed a cigar box as if it were a timepiece. "The words in you are, 'There is a place.'"

The cowboy thought that might be right.

"The place," said the longhaired man, walking now. Both his feet bare.

THE WOODS

They went into the heavy woods that walled the town. The long-haired man touched certain trunks in a knowing way. He said that every man he'd ever met had many names, and the truer a man worked to be, the more of his names he learned. He himself knew all his names but two. The name he was the most was Push Back, he said, owing to how the many peoples who'd made him had been pushed back, how pushing back was what his many peoples needed most to know.

The name he was the second-most was Pipe Hawk, owing to how he hawked the pipe or the pipe hawked him, meaning, Who filled and emptied who?

The name he was the least was Bill.

"It costs me," he said.

The cowboy asked him just who his peoples were because he sure looked awful white.

He said, "Cherokee, Choctaw, Chinese, Negro, Italian, Polish, Irish. In the summer, English."

They came upon a cave: a tremendous neckless rock licked with moss, foreheaded in saplings and shrubs. A slope led to its mouth where lips of fog slow-rolled. The fog stayed level, looking magic.

At the top of this slope Push Back unfolded a quilt the cowboy hadn't seen him carrying, in which was wrapped a lantern. He spread the quilt and sat facing the cave. "This place is for words," he said. He opened his cigar box: a pipe lay on a bed of strange black tobacco. He filled the pipe. "This place does not know words the way we know words."

He lit, drew a dry crackle, and passed the pipe, saying with smoke, "When you are in it you are its words."

The cowboy inhaled—smoke spread into his throat, a hot rash. He leaned into the feeling that followed. Not pleasure, but an oozy weakness near enough.

"The words already in you make you the words you are when you are in this place," said Push Back. He polished the lantern with his sleeve. "None of them words you know."

The cowboy held close to what he felt.

Push Back told a story about where the words that weren't known came from, how these words felt about where they came from, and under what conditions these words, without knowing why, turned into other words meant for other places. The story was long and lewd. It ended in a question the cowboy didn't hear all the way.

The cowboy answered that he didn't know about that but all the same was just sure as hell there was a way to make it right as he was about not knowing where that way was spending all its time like time was something free you didn't worry you'd run out of.

They passed the pipe four times.

THE CAVE

In lantern-light the walls revealed their stores of wealth: sparkling beads and strings and coins, cones and silver straws, ribbons, drapes, all of it cut in and by the breathing rock. The cowboy shivered in the cold. Push Back signaled to the standing figures that without moving rose, accidental statues massed by mineral drip into shapes the size of men, horses, train engines, struggling to look like what they weren't, and growing still.

THE WORDS

Push Back squatted by the hissing lantern, visible in its golden slashes. His hat gone, his hair oily.

The cowboy stayed some distance off in untouched darkness, sitting or standing, he couldn't say—he'd scrabbled further into the feeling of the pipe.

"What have you been?" said Push Back, his breath clouding. He sounded like a mad young man.

"A cowboy," said the cowboy.

"Where, where have you been?"

The cowboy touched his head, his hat gone too.

"Why?" said Push Back.

The cowboy patted his face. It was no longer swollen.

"Who, who, who?" screamed Push Back, bare-chested now.

The cowboy tried to point at himself.

Push Back stood, naked, his skin a being sprung from rock.

The cowboy tried to see any part of himself, his hands, his arms, his legs.

Push Back backed up. His mouth mouthed a word.

The cowboy touched himself all over—he wore nothing

too, not even boots. He didn't feel that he was where he was, but not being where he was was where he'd been, he remembered.

He felt the entrance of a long and mumbling fear. It reached for him.

Push Back, small and sucked-away, stopped. He raised the lantern. It went out with a whisper in the air.

The Veteran

The soldier was told, Go home.

He went home. On the way he became a veteran.

At home the veteran found sameness. This sameness was the same sameness he'd known before he'd left home for the base and the base for the war. Only now, the sameness no longer fit him. He tried to make the sameness fit him by tugging and squeezing it. He tried to fit the sameness by tensing and relaxing himself. Family, friends, girlfriends, and strangers tried to help him by declaring that the sameness fit him just fine, that he fit the sameness just fine, or by admitting that neither fit the other, not yet, and that if they could help, or help him help himself, please, let them know, tell them when or where or how.

Some never noticed his not-fitting. Some noticed but were afraid, angry, or disgusted.

He drank a glass of cold water in the kitchen. It was morning—morning in the glass of water, on the kitchen's tiles, and on the sliding glass door that opened to the green backyard where it was also morning, sparkling like crushed gems. His mother sat in the other room, trying not to listen. He set his empty glass next to other empty glasses in the dishwasher. Either his size had changed, or the size of the sameness had changed, or both, he decided.

He closed the dishwasher. In the other room, his mother turned the pages of the newspaper.

The veteran moved in with his girlfriend. His girlfriend changed her size to try to fit him, adjusting her dimensions every day, every hour, every moment. They made new or favorite meals for one another and ate at new or favorite restaurants. They watched or rewatched TV and movies. They read the same books. They rearranged her apartment. She asked about his not-fitting or didn't, depending on what she sensed he wanted, and later, on what she sensed he needed. Depending on what he sensed she wanted him to want or need, he responded with words too tight or too loose, a story or a statement that didn't match what either of them wanted. I love you, she said, when she hoped it might fit, but the veteran sensed that everything she did and didn't said I love you, and that it never fit.

He drank a glass of cold water in her kitchen. It was afternoon—afternoon in the glass of water, on her kitchen's tiles, and on the small window that looked into the alley where it was also afternoon, as long and flat as a map. He set the empty glass in the empty sink. His girlfriend sat upstairs in bed, making phone calls. It was his size that had changed, he decided.

His mother buzzed from downstairs.

The veteran moved in with his buddy, who wasn't a veteran. His buddy kept his size the size it'd always been, no adjustments, hoping that doing so would prompt the veteran's size into growing or shrinking back to where it used to be. They ordered pizzas and sandwiches and Chinese food. They played video games and board games and poker. They drank beer and liquor and smoked cigarettes and pot, and they burped and farted, and recalled the times they'd famously burped and farted in high school. Depending on their state, his buddy asked about the veteran's not-fitting, or the war, and the veteran would respond with words too loose or too tight, stories or statements that didn't match what it was that was between them, and the next day this exchange would seem embarrassing or inaccurate or meaningless, and only ever half-remembered.

He drank a glass of cold water in his buddy's kitchen. It was the middle of the night—the middle of the night in the glass of water, on the kitchen's tiles, and on the grimy window that faced another apartment's grimy window through which it was also the middle of the night, a night as shapeless as the sameness. He set the empty glass on the cluttered counter. His buddy played video games in the other room, talking trash to opponents hundreds or thousands of miles away. It was the sameness that wasn't the same, he decided.

He called his mother.

The veteran moved into his own apartment. He needed to decide: he didn't fit, or the sameness didn't fit, or both, or neither.

Or something else, he decided.

Or he didn't.

Or he did.

Or he watched TV and movies and porn, and himself masturbating.

Or he drank alcohol and energy drinks, and smoked cigarettes and cigars and joints.

Or he called family and friends and other veterans, veterans who had it better or worse.

Or he went out with exes and girls he knew from high school and girls he met in bars and on websites, and prostitutes.

Or he joined gyms and intramural sports and jogged and cycled and hiked and camped.

Or he painted and wrote and played instruments, and attended rallies.

Or he attended and left places of worship, and paid for psychologists and psychiatrists, and checked in and out of rehab, and was hired and fired and quit jobs, and became homeless, and committed suicide.

And whatever he did the sameness was not the same.

And he drank glasses of cold water in kitchens, where he waited for the time of day to turn up.

And he said to himself, Go home.

It Meant There Would
Be More

The girl I'd moved to Texas with sat beside me on our creaking feel-through futon. She squinted, thinking. I handed her a taco from the bag she'd brought.

She put the taco down and said, "Look here. I'm moving back to Illinois."

This was in our one-bedroom apartment, which for the last month had been my my-bedroom apartment. She'd been sleeping a block away with her books and her clothes and her papers, at Sujata's. My only demand, which we'd discussed, was lunch together when we weren't working. Hers, which we hadn't discussed, was "Look here" instead of "Hey honey" or "Oh sweetie," or the one we used to use when we used to take off each other's clothes, "Old bootsies."

"Old bootsies," I said. "When?"

She unwrapped the taco she'd put down: the foil, the steam, the smell of the meat. I knew she wouldn't eat it. I knew what she'd say, what I'd say, and the big feeling I'd soon be feeling. This big feeling I hadn't felt in a decade.

"Tomorrow," she said.

I quivered, but not with fear.

"Early in the morning," she said, as if saying, You're not sad about this, are you.

I said, "Tomorrow is my birthday," and then I felt it—the big feeling's fuzzy all-over tugging, pulling at my head and my spine and my heart, pulling until the pressure seemed to gently triple me, lifting me, placing me in what felt like equal wholes behind myself and upon myself and beyond myself.

She said some things I hardly heard. The futon creaked. I might have laughed.

"You aren't sad," she said, standing at the door with her purse.

My three whole selves and me looked at her at once. Through them, in her, I saw three months of sad shared space crushed by one month of hopeful separation into anger, an anger being ground right then by guilt into surrender. Able to stand, I stood. I touched my chest. I said that how I felt wasn't ever how I looked.

She left: the door, a blade of light, the door.

In me my three whole selves watched, waiting.

I cleaned. I scrubbed the kitchen sink and counter and bathroom sink and toilet, I took out the garbage, I vacuumed, I stripped my bedsheets and bagged my laundry, I showered—I peed and blew my nose and jerked off into the drain—I dressed, I brushed my teeth and flossed, I opened the fridge: a blade of light, a box of light, three cans of beer. I took the three cans of beer to my desk. My desk faced three windows that faced the apartment complex's small courtyard, a courtyard that was mostly dirty pool and banana trees. The windows, half-covered from above in canted wooden shutters, were unopenable. I opened all three beers. I drank them one by one as my neighbors, nonflamboyant gay men whose invitations to get together I regularly declined, gathered to lounge in the courtyard's plastic chairs, share cigarettes and joints, toss balls to their pit bulls and Chihuahuas, and tell stories I heard through my door's imperfect sealing in which the tellers proved to be heroes who nobly revealed the idiotic words, actions, and desires of idiotic others. None of this was what my three whole selves watched for. What my three whole selves watched for were omens. Omens were what their being there foretold. Night happened: the figures of my neighbors

faded, then their talk. I quit the desk, shed my clothes and boxers, and fell onto my sheetless bed. Sleep poured into the spaces
between my selves. I strained to stay awake; I strained to see past
the omen-vigil to the two times that all of this had happened before, once in high school when my brother had nearly died and
once in college when my brother had nearly died; I strained to see
to tomorrow morning, to the girl I'd moved to Texas with knocking on my my-bedroom apartment's door and saying, Way before
we moved to Houston.

With each other we can't be who we are.

But under that that's love.

That's love, under that?

That's why we waited and that's why we tried?

The overloaded cardboard boxes.

The long black road.

The rackety crash in the bathroom—I blundered naked out
of bed, dream-struck but awake, sure that the sound had happened. It had. The bathroom ceiling panel had fallen out of its
slot, dented the shower rod, and clattered into the tub. My toes
touched splintery bits of wood and flakes of plaster. I picked up
the little panel. With its knob-like handle it looked like the door
to a forgotten fairy-outhouse. Above me, what it had covered: a
dirty nest of pipes and ducts in a space too small for a shoe.

This was omen one. It meant there would be more.

Pleased, my three whole selves shook hands. They turned
away in smiling triumph. As they vanished, the big feeling in me
shrunk—buzzing with exhaustion, I staggered through darkness
to the futon to sit, to feel its pointy frame through the mattress,
to wait for the girl I'd moved to Texas with to knock on my door.
My eyes closed. She knocked on my door.

"I'm naked," I said, waking. Blades of light bristled in the
shaded windows.

She knocked again, not hard.

"Naked," I said, looking at myself. I stood. "In the buff. A-dangling!"

At my name I opened the door. She didn't want to laugh but did, and she took my hand and led me to the sheetless bed. We sat. She looked at the ceiling and then at the floor. "Way before we moved," she said. "We knew this."

I said that she was right: with each other we couldn't be who we were. We'd tried. We'd waited.

"You have a boner," she said, and touched it.

She kissed me and I kissed her back, and she pulled off her clothes but shushed me when I said "Old bootsies," and we went down on each other, and the sex we had stumbled from gentle to dirty-mean to sad. Neither of us came. We touched each other's sweating faces.

"This has nothing to do with love," she said.

"This," I said, indicating our embrace, "or this," I said, indicating the apartment, by which I meant our recent move-in and her right-now move-out.

She shook her head, meaning, You can't see it.

"Does it have to do with Sujata?" I said. "For you, I mean. For me it doesn't."

She kissed my forehead like a mom.

We loaded her station wagon with everything she hadn't already taken to Sujata's that would fit, which meant she left the bed, the futon, and the mostly empty bookshelf. We stood in the tenants' numbered parking spaces just over the courtyard's low fence, the pavement warm in Houston's casual February sunlight. Short-sleeves weather. I tapped the hood. "That's it?"

She handed me a wrapped box and for the second time that morning wished me happy birthday. "Don't open this until I'm gone," she said.

She said, "I'm going."

My chest condensed—I told her that the bathroom ceiling

panel had fallen, that if I'd been showering it would've cut my head and knocked me out and I might've nearly died.

She said she'd call me when she got to Little Rock.

I told her to call my brother when she got to Chicago, he could help her find a place in Logan Square again, and while she was at it could she see how he was doing, how was he doing, I wondered?

She'd been touching my arm until right then. "Look at you."

I looked at her. She was the sort of woman you felt in your throat, lean and strong in any light, her face a field of brightness. I took her hand, the one with the keys. I talked about what we were and what we could be.

She took back her hand. "When you talk about us you don't mean what you say."

"I mean it now."

"Exactly. That's it, that's all."

She dropped her keys on accident. I bent to grab them as she bent to grab them. She was crying, I was crying. She closed the door. She backed the station wagon into the street and onto a bottle, pop-crushing it, grinding it when she shifted to drive. None of these were omens. An omen is sensed with more than one sense in more than one place at once — the present, yes, but on top of that the past, a perch from where you're sure that everything beneath you is the future.

Across the street, hidden pigeons cooed in leafy live oaks. A man in a leather jacket and gym shorts walked an impatient dog while listening without speaking to his cellphone. Acorns skittered and crunched. I turned back, through the rusty black gate and into the courtyard.

Warren, my above-me neighbor with whom I shared a ceiling-floor, sat in a chair on the narrow porch-like space just outside his apartment. He lived on the second level of our two-level complex. From up there he'd watched every moment of the move-out. Every day, for hours, he watched every moment of as much as he could, and once a week he'd invite me up for lunch. "You don't eat lunch," he'd started saying.

I waved. He waved back with a travel mug.

When I got to my door it was locked. I'd locked it out of habit on the last load, which meant that a slice of me thought I was going with. The thought of a slice of me thinking I was going with hurt worse than hearing, "I'll call you when I get to Little Rock." I jiggled in the key and turned it. It broke.

I weighed the jagged half left in my hand. Omen two.

I tried the handle, which was still locked, and patted my pockets for my phone, which I'd left inside. I pinched at the key-shard in the lock. I patted my pockets. I tried the handle.

Warren said, "Angelo, do you like breakfast?"

He stood behind me in the courtyard, having come down the steps. A tall man tilting day by day into gray middle-age, lean except for a saddle-sized belly, which sagged. This close, I saw what was off about the way he stared: before and after speaking, he looked one second away from a wet belch.

I told him my key had broken in the lock and my phone was inside, and could he call Charlie?

He nodded purposefully. "Come with me."

I followed him up the stairs, past the porch-like space and through his apartment's open door. He phoned Charlie as we went. His place mirrored mine, with the same three windows and coarse carpeting and cutaway breakfast bar, but the arrangement of his matching furniture and paper-stuffed file cabinets segregated the space in such a way that it looked wholly unfamiliar, a different complex in a different city in a different state. Warren went to work behind the breakfast bar, the source of doughy-golden smells. I studied the series of framed charcoal sketches spaced out along the walls. All depicted meditative cowboys: cowboys alone or lonesomely together, cowboys before herds and canyons and cookfires. I got close to one of a roughed-up cowboy sitting on a crate in a cellar. He'd picked up a cracked guitar.

Warren caught me looking and smiled. His smile relieved him of his belch-face.

He said, "The city was the worst thing to happen to the cowboy."

"But the cowboy helped the city happen, didn't he?"

"That might be true where you're from."

We sat outside, the plates in our laps piled with blueberry-and-almond-piled waffles, everything gleaming in syrup. Warren told me he'd made the waffles from scratch and sliced the almonds himself, that the blueberries, syrup, and almonds were from Texas, the plates from Argentina. The more he spoke the more he sounded like a young man. I thanked him and chowed down.

"I have to tell you," he said, pointing at me with his fork, his elbow oddly high. "You look just so much like an old friend of mine. A very dear old friend."

By the way he said it, his dear old friend had been gone a long time. I imagined Warren as a young man holding another young man's hand in the middle of a dusty field, or beneath the long and reaching limbs of a live oak, or on the peeling seats of a stalled-out muscle car. I told him I was honored: I'd yet to look like anyone's dear old friend. The waffles were pasty, the syrup low-sugar, the almonds stale, and the blueberries frozen on the inside. I ate fast. I watched the parking lot, like Warren did every day, not for omens but for anything that might make me feel anything other than what I was feeling. I was feeling full of old cement.

Warren said, "Teresa looked like she wanted to stay."

I tried to hide my surprise at the fact that he knew her name by agreeing.

"From here, anyway," he said.

"What did I look like?"

"Like you were wondering what you looked like."

Charlie's truck rumbled into the two parking spaces marked MANAGER.

Warren took my plate, which I'd cleaned, and stacked it under his, which he hadn't touched. For the four months I'd lived there, Charlie's truck looked like it'd t-boned and been t-boned by two lesser vehicles, perhaps simultaneously, the dents somehow not deep enough to call for repair. I headed down the steps.

Warren waved the gift in his free hand. "Angelo, don't forget your . . . ?"

I told him what it was and went back up to take it.

"It's your birthday," said Warren, smiling.

Charlie shook my hand at my door. A white-bearded old man, he moved as thoughtfully as he spoke, his words dunked in West Texas twang. He drew tweezers from his shirt pocket and crouched at the doorknob. A man-sized gnome.

"Damn sorry about this," he said. "Predicament."

I said it was a minor inconvenience, no trouble.

"If you need to, you break lease. I'll fix it right for you."

By the time I realized he wasn't referring to the snapped key, he'd already extracted it, popped in a spare, and unlocked my door. I don't know how I didn't start crying again.

He straightened. "You try and have a nice day now."

"It's Angelo's birthday," said Warren as I closed my door.

My phone lay facedown on the coffee table between yesterday's bag of take-out tacos and the one that had been unwrapped. The tacos smelled as if they were trying hard to still be good. Teresa had texted, Sujata had texted, my brother had called twice.

Teresa's text read, did you open it?

Sujata's read, i am so sorry. do you want to talk? we talked too much maybe. but. come over if you want, okay?

My brother hadn't left any voicemails.

I sat on the futon and stared at the mostly empty bookshelf. I stared at the particleboard table we'd bought at Goodwill, at the drawer-less desk we'd found on the street, at the framed poster-sized photo of Lake Michigan she'd shot and developed herself, the water calm and long and blue, summer-shimmering. If I covered my face I could feel its cool breath. I covered my face. I thought, Maybe she left it behind on purpose. Maybe everything left behind is left behind on purpose. My phone buzzed—it was my mother—and as I declined the call, I heard brakes and barking rubber and an awful crunch.

I rushed outside, to the courtyard fence. Charlie's truck had been rear-ended by a U-Haul, the tailgate crushed up in an ugly kiss with the grille. An omen inside an omen.

Charlie climbed out steadily. He patted his pockets, like me.

"You all right?" I shouted.

He turned and bent to search the cab.

The U-Haul driver didn't leave his truck. He hid his face in his hands. Either his head was shaking his hands, or his hands were shaking his head. Sunlight razored off his silver watch.

"I'm calling the police," said Warren, pointing at his phone, calling the police.

Charlie found his phone and made a call.

In my apartment I listened to my mother's message. She sang happy birthday. My stepfather said to her, "Now?" then said loudly to the phone, "Going to spend your birthday shoveling snow, that's your present." My mother said it'd been coming down all night and seemed to have the nerve to come down all day too, just like the day you were born, if only you'd been born in Texas. She took that back. My stepfather said something I couldn't quite catch about trying to shovel snow with a lasso. Give a hug to Teresa, said my mother, I hope those buffoni at her job stop giving her the runaround, at your job too, and if not, don't worry, you won't be temping forever. I pray three times a day. If your brother forgets to call, call him.

Then she was alone, in another room. Sitting on their wide white bed. "Angelo," she said quietly, with conspiratorial gravity. "When I woke up this morning, you know what I saw first thing?"

"I do," I said.

"On the window, in the frost."

"A pair of wings," I said as she said, "A pair of wings."

She whispered, "You're watched over."

I sat at my desk, opened the blinds a little, and texted my brother: i don't want to be watched over.

Another from Sujata: wait, don't come over. bad. let me get you lunch. guadalupana?

Another from Sujata: beer lunch at hay merchant?

Another from Teresa: you won't, will you.

Another knock at the door: I opened it to Jonas, a handsome young fellow in his mid-twenties, my neighbor with whom I shared a wall. Mostly I heard him more than saw him, his buoyant laughter bobbing through the walls at all hours, pulling with it the lesser laughter of his friends and boyfriends. Teresa had said that he was clocking in and out on his good looks, that when he one day found he had only so much left it'd be too late for him to learn a new way of working. I'd disagreed too strongly. She'd said, You *can* see it.

Jonas held a stack of slim books. "You check this shit out?" he said, motioning to the accident. He said the man in the U-Haul had stayed in his seat to bang the window with his head. "Listen."

A faint tap tap tap. An omen.

Laughing, Jonas handed me the books. "Tell Teresa she's helped me express myself."

Everything in the stack was poetry: chapbooks, collected works, a few she'd had the poet sign. More than once she'd sworn to me she'd stop lending, that too many of her favorites had never made it back. To hide my surprise I said, "You liked them?"

"Dude, I wrote all night, I'm writing this epic love poem to Montrose. I got to where it was like I was inside the poem—you know what I mean?—but kind of outside the poem at the same time, cheering myself on and shit. It was cool. It was like I was close enough to give myself a reacharound." He plucked a hand-rolled cigarette from behind his ear. "Smoke?"

We stood in front of our doors, directly beneath Warren's second floor porch-space. A cop the size of a professional wrestler escorted the U-Haul driver to his squad car. The driver wobbled, his face tucked as close to his armpit as possible. From that angle it was tricky to tell much about him—his age and his race, his build, and was he even a dude? Charlie, sitting in the driver's seat with the door open, chewed his lip. Jonas took a drag and handed the cigarette to me. I hadn't had a smoke since Teresa had moved to Sujata's. I pulled hard. It was a joint.

"It's Angelo's birthday," said Warren above us, unseen.

Jonas told a story about a birthday party he'd attended, drunk and on E, in the back of a U-Haul. They'd taken turns tooling the thing around a forest preserve while everybody in the trailer danced in strobe lights to deafening house music. His little brother had brought fireworks. "I lit a roman candle between my legs," he said. "All night I blew glowing loads."

He laughed at this and made a note on his phone.

A convertible zipped up and jerked to a stop across the street. A fuming woman got out, dressed for office work, not for moving boxes. She talked to the cop, then marched to the U-Haul. A breeze brought her perfume to us: the smell of an older woman or an older time. Doors banged. Charlie drove away, the cop drove away, and the woman, behind the wheel of the U-Haul, turned the key. A whiny wheeze. A sound the woman seemed incapable of making.

We moved to the plastic chairs beneath the banana trees. The sun's spread had shifted — it freckled the surface of the dirty pool. Warren nodded from above, leaning on the rail. He now wore a cowboy hat.

"I'm thirty-one," I said, though no one had asked.

Jonas told a story about the first thirtysomething he'd ever dated, a conservative self-hating drug dealer named Freddie, who'd treated him with less respect than the average man would give to a stranger's turd. A few months after they'd broken up, Jonas was walking home toasted from the bar when he spotted Freddie's pickup parked in front of a fire hydrant, windows down. "I called it in. That is, after I took a shit on the driver's seat."

Warren said, "When I was thirty-one I was living in Chicago. I'm from California."

"Where in Chicago?" I said.

"Naperville."

A tow truck backed up towards the U-Haul. Its bony driver popped out and lowered the rig. The fuming woman, on her phone, stood as if she knew how to crush whatever happened next. She appeared to be in her late twenties, mid-thirties, or early forties, depending on the angle. I squinted, like Teresa, and that's when she met my stare — in her fury I saw no shadows, only painful light on light. She held our eye contact hard while speaking loudly in a language I didn't recognize. Embarrassed, and embarrassed at being a bit aroused, I lost our staring contest. Out of the corner of my eye I watched her walk behind the trucks.

Jonas told a story, and then another story, and then another. I listened to the weed I'd smoked crinkle my spine and my head and my heart. I didn't feel tripled. I felt divided, the portions unequal and vague. I catalogued the omens: the fallen bathroom panel, the broken key, the crash, the crash's kiss-like tangle, the tap tap tap of the driver's head, the fuming woman's gaze. Did these omens argue that my future had my number? That I had no role in my future's making? That my future was already making of me what it pleased?

I thought, Maybe such things are only true in retrospect. Or always. Always true in retrospect. I folded my hands behind my head: the rotating shade, the hot slash of full light.

The gate slammed. Eduardo strolled in, built like a cylinder, a friendly piston of a man. He'd invited me to have a beer in the courtyard more than all my other neighbors combined. Any time he said hello it sounded like a clap on the back. He was squarely in his thirties. In one hand he walked his big sweet dog, Lady, and in the other he carried a case of Shiners. When he saw me, he let go of the leash and pretended to have an acid flashback.

"Man, is that Angelo?" he talk-shouted, his normal tone. "No way that's Angelo! Angelo keeps his door closed, Angelo doesn't answer when you knock—no no no, I'm seeing shit!"

Lady jammed her head between my legs. I let her. I scratched her ears.

Warren took off his cowboy hat and said it was my birthday. He seemed sad.

Eduardo cheered my name and tossed beers to everyone but Warren. He took the chair between me and Jonas and asked me what was new, how was work, Teresa?

Everyone waited for me to say she'd moved out. Including Eduardo.

"She moved out," I said.

He said he was sorry to hear it. "You love her?"

I said I did. That I meant it, though, felt shameful.

If I loved her, why had I let her leave?

"Can't help who we love," said Eduardo, his resignation humble. "Only how."

Jonas laughed.

Eduardo said, "My sisters haven't talked to me in ten years."

Still laughing, Jonas began a story about how pathetically long it took him to move out of his first boyfriend's minivan and how fucked up it was that the situation he'd landed in was so much worse than the situation he'd run away from, and maybe because what Jonas was saying seemed more real than anything I'd ever heard him say before or since, I interrupted him to tell Eduardo that Teresa had hated the job and hated Houston, she'd hated the strip malls and parking lots and potholey streets, the double whammy of douchey car culture and douchey business culture, not to mention guns and megachurches and humidity, and worst of all, she hated who we were when we were here. It took me a long time to say this. Jonas had stopped his story.

Eduardo handed me another beer. "At least it wasn't somebody else got between you." The way he said it, he was giving me an opening.

Jonas moaned, "Old bootsies!"

I leaned forward. Jonas had squeezed his face into a constipated approximation of sexual passion. He banged his chair's arms and squealed, "Don't stop, old bootsies, don't stop . . . !" He groped an invisible me.

"Man, that's not cool," said Eduardo. "But yeah, we heard it."

Warren put on his hat and left. It made me want to hug him.

" . . . you stopped," said Jonas breathlessly.

The performance over, he slapped at the air and laughed — I noticed for the first time that when not filtered through a wall, his laughter had a toxic edge. "I'm sorry," he said, "but you had to be talking too. What sort of shit were *you* saying?"

"I was reciting shitty epic love poems," I said. "I stay up all night shitting them out."

Jonas just smiled. He tapped a note into his phone.

I stood. I said I'd be back, and passed through the gate and onto slanting root-ravaged sidewalks. I walked down Pacific, past the rainbow-flagged gay bars and dance clubs, then crossed Fairview into Montrose's northern edge, the old homes coming down and the snazzy condos going up. Nothing was an omen. Not the flowering bushes that lazed through tall gates, or the dead palm trees that stood like extinguished torches, or the parked car with dozens of action figures glue-gunned to its hood, or the balcony populated with rhinestone-peppered mannequins holding one another's hands, or the two old women on a driveway in lawn chairs using straws to drink from beer cans, or the rotting possum caught in the crack of a rotting fence, or the fact that just before the sun squeezed out on the horizon I was standing in front of Sujata's. She lived on the second floor of an old house cut up into apartments. All month I hadn't come by once. I'd come by way too many times in the months before, sometimes alone. When we were alone we always nearly kissed. I buzzed up.

Her boyfriend Patrick said through the speaker, "Angelo?"

He didn't live there but he often spent the night. During the day he helped the newly blind adjust to service dogs, learn Braille, and find jobs. He wasn't blind himself, but his voice worked the spirit like a deep massage worked the body. It was strong and velvety. For years he'd voice-acted in locally produced religious radio dramas. He'd played almost every apostle.

His voice made me more aware of myself. I was no good to anyone.

"We've been worried," he said.

I put my head on the door. Everything he said, I'd hear later. His voice was that astounding.

He said, "Is Sujata with you?"

"Where did she go?" I asked.

"She said she was meeting you at the bar. Come on up! I'll call her again."

The door buzzed unlocked. I opened it, let it close, and left, walking fast and checking my phone.

Sujata: at hay merchant

Sujata: drunk

My brother: ha dude mom says the same shit to me. i bet to everyone. i'll call you soon, you won't believe my day. i don't know how i'm not in the hospital

My brother: seriously

My brother: oh shit, i just got it, you must be seeing shit again!!! OMENSS

My brother: looking forward to what the fuck you saw today i hope this time it teaches you something

My brother: actually fuck learning, i hope this time it makes you actually do something, something different

My brother: by which i mean happy birthday little baby waby angel wings

Teresa: i want you to open it. right now.

I stumbled as I read the texts, the glow dizzying me whenever I looked back to the smashed-up sidewalks. Everything lurched and I lurched with it.

Happy voices met me as I returned to the complex's courtyard. The gate was propped open. I walked in and around, and where I'd been sitting sat Sujata. She sat like she was waiting to be seen. She wore clothes one might wear to bed. When she looked at me I felt terrible and then terrific, and then terrible, and then terrific. In her I saw what I'd been seeing in her since we met: who I'd once wanted to be, not who I was.

"I'm telling them what you were like in college," she said, very drunk.

Eduardo grinned as if the solution to my situation had been handed to him, beer-like, and all that was left was for him to open it and pass it on to me. "Man, I don't believe it! Angelo the party-monster-animal, Angelo the Romeo. I can see that, the Romeo. But not puking in a cab."

Meanwhile, Jonas tapped away at his phone. He mouthed

words, his handsome face enchanted in the screen's pale glow. Alone but not lonesome, he seemed to be casting a spell on himself. It made me angry.

"I told him about the time you stripped to ring tones on the Red Line," said Sujata.

I said that there were worse things that were even funnier and then I said I had to use the bathroom. Sujata said that she should too, she'd been holding it. Eduardo just about applauded.

I locked the door behind us and sat on the futon. She stood, watching me. She stepped closer. Space popped and snapped. She was the kind of woman who, just by being near you, made you certain that you could be who you wanted to be.

But after you became that you, would it be boring to you both?

And after you broke up, would guilty longing bring you both back?

Under that, was that love?

She shook her head. I saw her seeing in me what she always saw, another shot, one she felt she had to take, and I knew then that this moment was what the omens had brought, that this was how their happening was answered, and whether anyone had anything to do with it or not, my end of what happened after this would be up to me, would make me make it mine.

To sit beside me she moved Teresa's gift to the coffee table. It was wrapped in the Christmasy paper we'd used two months ago. Whenever I asked Teresa about things she thought I ought to remember, she said, Think. I looked at her gift on the coffee table. I thought.

Sujata took my hand. I touched her arm. We'd been here before, tempted between our breakups. We'd dated eight years ago for two years at the University of Chicago, then a year later for one year after graduation. When I found out I was moving to Houston she'd been in grad school at Rice for three years.

"It's a sign!" she'd said when I'd called, when I'd asked her to help us find an apartment. "We can be friends. You have a girlfriend, I have a boyfriend. Friends friends friends, the four of us!"

"It's a sign," she'd said the first time we were alone at her place, in the kitchen, at the table, on the couch, wanting to touch.

That night I'd said that signs were us seeing ourselves, that we saw the parts of ourselves we wanted badly to be there. She'd said I had it mostly wrong, that if you saw it it was there, there for you to take.

The futon creaked. I touched our hands with my other hand. So did she.

She said, "I could say I'm sorry. I could say I don't know. We know it's a bad idea, but is it the only idea we have?"

"I don't know," I said. "I'm sorry."

We kissed. Our mouths fit like before, and like before I didn't feel as if I had anything to do with it though I knew I did. Then we were standing. Then we were in bed, naked except for underwear. My body stank of sweat. Her breath was like an old man's clothes. We pushed and we pulled at each other's limbs, and when I went down on her, she stopped me. She was crying.

Then she was sleeping. I set my head on her shoulder.

I woke to knocking at the door.

I sat up. Sujata was gone and so were my boxers. The clock read quarter to three. The knocking was patient, steady, and firm, with intervals. I didn't feel patient, steady, or firm, and I didn't feel inside of any intervals. I touched my chest. Dread wheeled, a slow and anxious turning. Its edges churned up guilt and regret and a madness for forgiveness, for willful confrontation, for confessions and repentance and confirmation.

I felt certain that I would act. The certainty widened my dread.

I stepped out of bed and onto Sujata, who was asleep on my laundry bag. She grunted and I fell—I whacked my head on the corner of the footboard. Mumbling, she climbed over me and onto the mattress, carrying an armful of my dirty clothes.

The knocking continued.

In pain I walked across the apartment and pressed my ear to the door. At every knock I blinked, the sound a blade in my head. In the interval I switched ears and noticed blood—I was bleeding down my cheek and chin, bleeding onto the door, bleeding onto the carpet. The more blood I touched, the more blood there was. It didn't seem possible that I could be its source.

The knocking continued.

I said, "It's me."

The knocking stopped mid-knock.

"It's me," I said, louder.

A righteous voice said, "Angelo."

I remembered to act: I opened the door.

One of the Days
I Nearly Died

When it was happening I was alone. I didn't think of my wife, of how she and I suspected she was pregnant (she wasn't, but by the time the period came we'd both said a brace of big ugly honest things that had made the other think, These big ugly honest things you've said are who you Really Are, when really the big ugly honest things were only who we'd clubbed each other into becoming for a one-month spell inside a six-year spell that up until then had us living on Logan Boulevard in Logan Square thinking we'd be local, organic, and happy right up until we died blissful simultaneous deaths in the final scene of the epic film of our active old age, or at least that's how I remember it out loud when I apologize, and when I see my ring on my finger in a mirror, and when I slam dishwasher drawers and shout, Listen! You aren't listening!), and I didn't think of my pray-hard mother, who expected me and my wife for dinner, for our family's weekly Family Dinner Night in the house I grew up in in Western Springs, homemade raviolis, and I didn't think of my brother who didn't at the time go to our family's weekly Family Dinner Nights because he was way away in another state (Texas) with a woman we all liked (she liked him) and he for some reason didn't, a woman he'd tried for four years to trick himself into thinking he liked so that he could trick himself into thinking he loved, despite how he felt compelled to act in front of her in front of us, despite every big ugly honest thing I ever said to him when we were so deep in drinking at the Map Room that we with old-timey windups pitched each other's phones at the wall, and I didn't think of my dad who was dead, six years dead, dead and in the dead place where if I died there in the Loop in my car alone (which it looked like I would) I'd be too, doing this probably, and I didn't think of my dopey dingdong stepdad who to this day doesn't know how to think of anybody other than my mother, which we should appreciate but don't. No. What I thought of was the other day I'd nearly died. The other day wasn't much like the day that made me think of it, I think. The other day had only a little bit of something pinched inside it. But it was long. Because it was long and you were in it, in it like the little bit of something, you were made to laugh at yourself, or at yourself laughing. It was the kind of day that made you think that thinking about the things that mattered was what mattered.

Was where you were what mattered?

We Try to Find the Spring in Spring Rock Park in Western Springs, Illinois

We try to find the spring in Spring Rock Park in Western Springs, Illinois, and we can't. We can't remember. We can't remember where it isn't anymore.

We stomp out of Spring Rock Park and we cross the train tracks where we're not supposed to cross and we pass the new train station made to look like the old train station and we get right up to the Western Springs Water Tower. The first floor of the Western Springs Water Tower houses the Western Springs Historical Society, we remember. We knock on the door and we try to open it and it's locked—we all try one at a time, once—and we try the windows, all of them, all of them locked. We cup our faces to peek through the windows: inside it's dark, the darkness looking thick and poured. Outside where we are it's summer afternoon, linked ponds of light, earthy-cool islands of shade. We sit in the grass of the Western Springs Water Tower Green in the Western Springs Water Tower's bending bridge of shadow. We sit in an arrangement that would like to be a circle. We're thirsty.

A clean police car rolls by. In it the officer watches us, not the road. The road is Grand Avenue. We remember Grand Avenues.

While the officer watches us and not the road he runs a stop sign.

We toss off our shoes and we pick our ears and we pretend to know where we really are. We hurt in places and in ways we can't help each other find. These places and these ways, they groan from where they hide—they're walls about to give, floors about to split, hearts about to starve. They're how we mope along alone together. They're why we want to find the spring in Spring Rock Park that we can't remember where it isn't anymore.

The Western Springs Water Tower anyone can find for now. It's tall and even more alone than us, with a splendid limestone body and a splendid redbrick head and a splendid short and slant-ing roof that once was struck like a match by a strip of light-ning, we remember. Without moving, the Western Springs Wa-ter Tower laps at the fluids of the last two centuries with the kind of lips and tongue we can't imagine, tasting no one we know can remember what.

Its tank is empty, we remember.

Two smart mothers push strollers stuffed with babies and baby-things right by us. They don't look our way on purpose, none of them. This is a way and a place in which we hurt.

Remember! one of us says, the oldest, and the way it's said is fury from a deathbed.

Remember? says the youngest. Remember what? Remember how?

The shade outside our shade shifts its many edges.

Remember with saying so, says the one who says so little.

Saying so? we say.

We think about it. We feel it out.

A Say-So, we say, remembering.

A firetruck chugs past, no lights or sirens on. In it the fire-fighters watch the road, not us.

So we do it.

We Say-So about the spring.

We say, The tribesmen and tribeswomen who first found the spring found it speaking from a rock. What it said, it seemed to say to all: We are we are we are we are.

Winter and summer, fall and spring, We are.

You don't say, says the oldest.

We say, The tribesmen and tribeswomen drank from it. They hunted the animals that drank from it and they gathered from the plants and the trees that drank from it. They moved away from it and they moved back to it. The stories they told of it told of the ones who to them had made it. To them the stories seemed to say, We are you we are you we are you we are you.

This we don't remember, we say.

We say, The settlers who first found the spring found it speaking from a rock. What it said, it seemed to say to them: I am here.

Winter and summer, fall and spring, I am here.

If you say so, says the oldest.

We say, The settlers built a little house around the spring. They built little roads from the little house to bigger roads. They caught the spring's water in buckets and jars and jugs. The stories they told of it told of what to them it might make of their settlement. To them the stories seemed to say, You are here.

This we remember, we say.

A police officer rides by on a bright bicycle. Watching us, he steers with a jerk onto the sidewalk, crunching to powder a nub of colored chalk left there by a child. He dismounts near a memorial bench.

We say, The tribesmen and tribeswomen returned.

Some tribesmen were impressed by the creations and arrangements set inside the little house, by the way the settlers took the spring's water into buckets and jugs, and these tribesmen asked questions, while other tribesmen were outraged, afraid, or squeamish, and made dark jokes the interpreters did not interpret.

Some settlers were impressed by what to them was the tribesmen's curiosity or indifference, and they answered questions with their own questions, which nourished more questions, while other settlers were squeamish, afraid, or outraged, and made dark jokes the interpreters did not interpret.

The tribesmen and tribeswomen departed.

The settlers caught the spring's water in jugs and drums and tanks.

The settlers named their settlement Western Springs, we say.

The tribesmen and tribeswomen returned with kindred tribesmen and tribeswomen from nearby lands and together discussed the likelihood of an upcoming great departure.

Some tribesmen from this discussion departed to meet with other more important settlers in Chicago, and upon their return, met again with the settlers of Western Springs at the little house. Through interpreters the tribesmen described the Chicago promises that signaled, it was true, an upcoming great departure to other lands and springs.

One settler asked if this meant they'd never return?

One tribesman told a story of the tribe that walked into the sky.

One settler told a story of the executed god-man whose body returned to life.

One settler added, And walked into the sky.

One tribesman said a spring is an always-returning.

Visit, said one settler.

The same police car pulls up. Two officers get out and join the officer who's leaned his bicycle against the bench. They all adjust their loaded belts.

We say, The tribesmen invited the settlers to a ceremony of singing, dancing, and storytelling, and although the interpreters did not interpret on account of their participation, the settlers, who did not participate, made do with meaning on their own.

The tribesmen departed and never returned.

The settlers pounded a plaque into a rock.

The police officers approach.

The settlers built more and bigger roads to more and bigger

houses. They built a railroad. They built sewers and wells and drove them deep into the earth.

Then the spring stopped speaking, we say.

All its water was gone.

Its little house fell down.

The police officers stop outside our would-be circle. Their faces are practiced.

We say, as loud as we can, And it never spoke again.

Leave, say the police officers.

This we don't remember, I say.

I don't and you don't, you say.

He doesn't. She doesn't.

So we say, They don't.

Western Avenue

A young woman moves into her first apartment in the city on Western Avenue.

"West of what?" says her mother, irritated.

They're eating hot dogs and sitting on tape-sticky boxes. The floor, walls, and ceiling smell like feet and smoke.

The young woman says, "The lake."

They check a map on her phone. Neither has been to the lake.

"But look at all these other streets," says her mother. "They're more western than Western. Just look at them."

They hug goodbye on the sidewalk. The young woman's mother has gone from irritated to aggravated. "Forget it," she says, tearing up, "forget everything," and she walks around the block to where she's parked her emptied car. The young woman lights a cigarette. She tries to see the people in the cars in the traffic.

The young woman moves into her second apartment in the city on Western Avenue.

"I'll do it tomorrow," says her boyfriend, who's moved in with her. They're naked on a frameless mattress. He touches her legs. She feels impatient: he isn't saying he wants to break up, he isn't breaking up, and he isn't working like she is to make things bigger, deeper, or brighter. He's on the other side of a fence she hadn't known was there.

The young woman moves into her third apartment in the city on Western Avenue.

"Cowboy Avenue!" says her roommate from Missouri, riding an imaginary horse in the kitchen.

"Yee-fucking-haw!" says her roommate from Indiana, driving imaginary cattle from the loveseat.

"Giddyup giddyup giddyup, son!" says her roommate from Michigan, humping an imaginary cowboy against the entertainment center.

The young woman, who's from Illinois, laughs more than she has laughed since high school and drinks more than she has drunk since college and works more than she has ever worked at any time. When she isn't laughing, drinking, or working, she feels a frozen wave inside herself. It's standing still and shrinking.

Or it's not that it's shrinking, it's that the vast black beach it's landed on is more immeasurable than she supposed.

Either way the wave is hard to reach, even when she feels it.

She feels it less.

She tries to settle the matter but can't. She looks for ways to talk about being unable to settle the matter, but with words she reaches only other reaching words, and her attempts leave her impatient, irritated, and immobile. She feels like a fence seen from faraway.

She moves into her fourth apartment in the city on Western Avenue with her fiancé.

"Tomorrow?" says her fiancé.

She moves into her fifth, sixth, and seventh apartments in the city on Western Avenue alone.

She lives above laundromats and banks and liquor stores and next to used car lots and carwashes and car repair shops, and when she thinks about what it will take to move again, she walks across her floors and under her ceilings and between her walls to her windows, from where she looks or listens to Western Avenue, feeling always that it's only ever where she's left it.

Dead Dogs

That winter, every other man or woman I met when I brought my then-fiancée's dog to the dog-friendly bar would tell me about a dog they'd had, a dog who was dead. They'd be petting my then-fiancée's dog. They'd stop.

"Dead for how long, now?" they'd sometimes say to themselves.

"Dead a long time," they'd sometimes answer.

The dog-friendly bar was an Irish pub with a Gaelic name so thicketed in consonants that I never heard anyone in it or the neighborhood call it anything other than "the Tab." The neighborhood was Rogers Park, as far north and east as you could be and still be in the city, an hour and then some by train or by bus from everyone I was used to knowing. I lived with my then-fiancée and her dog in a squeaking fourth floor apartment on Chase and Sheridan. If I'd somehow stood on the roof I could've hurled a baseball into the lake, though all we saw from the windows was other people's windows.

That winter my then-fiancée flew to Europe for five weeks. During those five weeks I walked the four blocks to the Tab with her dog nearly every night. Until then I'd never been a regular anywhere. The Tab was shoebox-shaped and dim with a sour-water stink that stuck to what you wore until you washed it twice. Up front you'd find two sloping pool tables and three ragged dartboards and one ledge-like stage where loaded would-be stand-up comics tried twice weekly to make you believe that they didn't believe in themselves on purpose. Its crowd, unlike the mostly white crowds I'd seen in the bars of Wicker Park and Logan Square, was white and black and brown all over, old and young, everywhere from shit-your-pants-miserable to shit-your-pants-satisfied. They sat at the same tables to watch the same games and shout the same objections, and when they met my then-fiancée's dog they told me their dead dog stories, every one of which was different.

Their names and the names of their dead dogs dissolved as soon as I heard them. Their stories, for reasons I'm still failing to find, stacked up in me like coarse little stones.

"He used to lie on the last step," said the regular with the dented head, the one who the more he drank the less drunk he looked. He pointed, imagining. "I still walk high over it. Every morning I do."

I bought him a drink. Everyone who told me about their dead dog, I bought them a drink. I didn't think too much about why. I had a job, low rent, no debt. I had a fiancée in Europe. I had a dog. The dog had a name my then-fiancée's ex-boyfriend had picked, and whenever I said it that winter I thought about her in Europe hanging out with this ex-boyfriend "as friends" (they were attending the same series of conferences with the same reunited network of former graduate school classmates) while I was here hanging out "as friends" with her dog, who she'd started calling "our dog," whose name was Burnham. Burnham was an eager ninety pounds, all fluff and muscle, a collie-colored collie-German shepherd mix with a perky nose and flip-floppy ears. He was everything I then knew about dogs. I had never wanted, owned, or watched a dog. That winter I watched Burnham poke at whatever came before him with his nose and mouth and tongue, sniffing and licking, snuffling, and although I never said it out loud I loved the way he loved everyone who let him touch them. It was hard for me to love anyone that winter. That was maybe why I bought so many drinks for so many people I'd just met.

"We forgot to ask somebody to watch her when we left," said the long-bearded bartender. "My dad thought my mom had taken care of it, my mom thought my dad had. So she was in the apartment totally alone for a week. They didn't realize the fuckup until we were on the way back, but when we opened the door the dog was just sitting there by the shoe-pile looking happy, like all we'd done was go around the corner for a pop. She hadn't shat anywhere we could find it. She hadn't even pissed. All she ate was a box of oat bran."

I bought him a drink.

"You didn't see me drinking more than one," he said, drinking.

"German shepherds, now they got noses," said the young woman with the brightly dyed buzzcut. She came up from rubbing Burnham's muzzle. "The one I grew up with, when she smelled weed, she howled like the whole city was on fire again and every drop in the lake wouldn't put it out. Whenever I was coming home high, I snuck in through the window and made straight for the shower. My big sister, she used to smoke before she got got by Jesus, she knew, she'd play Momma and wait with the dog in the bathroom for me. Soon as the dog started barking, she started slapping me."

I bought her a drink.

She said, "You smoke?"

I said I used to.

"Weed," she said.

I said I used to, and I tried to make it sound like I'd known what she'd meant.

She nodded like she understood. I bought her another drink. She got up to use the bathroom and didn't come back.

"This one's a real softie, I can tell," said the moustached middle-aged man, well-dressed, "but holy hell, you should've got a load of the sorry mutt I used to have, was he a dope. It was embarrassing how submissive he was. He'd lie down for anything. Little dogs. Cats. Remote control cars. The thing was, though, he was huge and his hair was black, thick and black, and he had an even blacker face. So what do you think happened? What happened was everybody thought he was mean, bad, scary, that he'd bite your ass off. Black's got these symbolical meanings in our society and boy did I see it. I'm no racist, that's for sure."

I bought him a drink.

He bought me a drink.

"You a fag?" he said.

I said I wasn't.

"Me neither."

"This guy I was dating, I watched his dog once," said the young woman in the UIC hoodie. Although she was right out of college or right about to be, how she sat at the bar had her seeming older. She looked familiar, maybe, like someone I'd forgotten? She picked up her drink to put it on a coaster. "He had to go to Michigan for his uncle's funeral. Him and his uncle were close, it was sad. I watched the dog for the weekend. Twice a day I walked him on the beach, Lane Beach Park, where everybody lets their dogs off leash, you know all about it I'm sure. So me and the dog come up to these three beefsteaky dudes walking four dogs, all off-leash. I look at the dudes, I give them the Is It Okay If My Dog Plays with Your Dogs? look, but I'm wearing sunglasses and they're wearing sunglasses, and it seems like they see me, like it's okay, so I let my dog go bounding up and before I know what's happening their dogs fan out. They surround my dog. One of them pounces—he's got my dog's neck-fur in his mouth, he's growling, and my dog's laying down all submissive, and the other dogs, still circling, they start growling too. I'm freaking out. I'm worried these dogs are going to send my dog to the hospital or worse. So I'm like, 'Can you get your dog off my dog like right fucking now, please?' and the owner, who isn't even looking at me, he says to his dog, 'LET GO,' and his dog lets go but doesn't move, he starts barking these ugly barks. I'm about to say something else when the owner steps up and kicks his dog in the head. He just fucking boots him. It hardly does anything to the dog but it stuns me, like he kicked me too, and the next thing I know my dog is up and running, he's *running away*. I sprint after him screaming for him to stop but he isn't stopping, he's running off the beach and towards the parking lot, and then he's *in* the parking lot, he's running between the rows of cars, he *runs into the street* — into Sheridan, you know how busy Sheridan is — and a cabbie slams the brakes and gets rear-ended by the cabbie behind him, and tires are screeching and I'm screeching and there's horns and shouting and horrible crunching sounds, and as I'm watching all of this, I watch the whole thing, the dog somehow makes it to the other side of the street alive. Holy fuck. I'm out of breath and sobbing, my legs are dead, but I can see on the other side of the street there's this tall old man with a cane. He calls out — the dog runs right up to him and stops. Like that was all I had to do. I cross the street, I'm blubbering, I don't know how *I* don't get hit, I leash the dog and thank the tall old man a million times and explain what happened, and he just smiles and says, 'Darling, what I did didn't require much.' I give him a hug. I give hugs all the time but I mean the shit out of this one. Then one of the cabbies stomps over, he's furious, he's pointing at me. The tall old man raises his cane and tells the cabbie to go back to his car. And he does."

I bought her a drink.

"Your dog is really big," she said, scratching Burnham's back. His tail swished between us. "Little men with big dogs make me feel bad for the dogs. I'm glad you're not a little man."

"I didn't even tell those assholes that they were assholes," she said.

She bought me a drink.

I bought her another drink.

"I'm leaving too," she said, when I got up to go.

She waved down the long-bearded bartender. Her friends, laughing at a nearby table, didn't have whatever she had that made her seem older. They smiled at me in a way I hadn't seen in a long time. Burnham tugged towards them. I let him say hello.

"Awwwww," they said, and the drunkest one, whose drunkenness I didn't like at all, took pictures of him with her phone.

I walked the young woman to the Red Line stop at Jarvis, past ATMs and shuttered liquor stores and plowed troughs of old snow. The wind was big. We kept bumping into each other, our coat-sleeves scritching. Powdery flakes stung our faces. As we came to the station, a train left for the Loop, ding-donging its doors closed. The rumbling track chipped off blue sparks into darkness. Burnham licked the lower rim of a trash can.

She bent to pet him. Her grin was warm and wide and patient. It wasn't that I knew her from somewhere, I realized. It was that I wanted to.

"What a lucky dog," she said, fluffing Burnham's sides. "What a lucky dog to have. I didn't ask you, how long have you had him?"

I watched her, waiting, and when she looked up over the dog at me I said that my fiancée had had him for two years. I tried to act like it wasn't lousy and low-down to fail to mention my fiancée until right then. She tried too.

"Later," she said.

"We're walking late," said the dreadlocked middle-aged man, "and this other brother he's walking towards us, and my dog, his hair raises and he bares his teeth and he starts snarling something nasty. My dog was a monster, a hundred and twenty pounds all the way to the grave, made somebody shake every day. This brother, he stops a safe distance away, he goes, 'Man, what's wrong with your dog?' I go, 'Man, what's wrong with *you*? My dog here's saying you're the one with the problem, so unless you want him to specify, you better get on over to the other side of the street.'"

I bought him a drink.

He tapped the bar and said, "*You're* the one always buys everybody drinks in here."

I said I was sometimes.

He lowered his voice in a comic way. "You know that doesn't make you generous."

I said I knew what he meant. But I didn't.

"You're not even thirty, are you."

I said I would be soon.

He clapped as if I'd made a joke, and with pretend-gravity ordered me and the pink-haired bartender shots. "To Mr. Soon being 'soon'!" he shouted. We downed them. He motioned for the pink-haired bartender to refill our glasses. When we raised them again he said, "Your turn to toast, Mr. Soon."

I don't remember what I said, but whatever it was, it wrecked the moment.

That night Burnham didn't eat his dinner. I'd been feeding him whenever we got back from the Tab, filling his bowl at seven or ten or two, and he'd been gobbling it up right away. This time he just stood there. I just stood there too, tottering, more drunk than usual. He sniffed at the bowl's lip, lay down beside it, and put his head on his paws. He looked bored. This irritated me. It seemed ungrateful. I changed into pajamas and got into bed and opened my laptop. Burnham followed me into the bedroom and flopped out on the rug with a pouty sigh.

In bed I read emails from my then-fiancée. The emails were dense with details about the famous people in her field she'd been meeting, how they were personable or insufferable, how she and her ex-boyfriend were having a fine time as friends, how her ex-boyfriend's new girlfriend (who'd taken quite a lot of time off to travel with him, she noted) was polite and smart if not a little bland, how good the food, beer, wine, and spirits were, how so much of what she'd eaten and drunk had given her ideas for the wedding, and speaking of that had I looked into those caterers because if we didn't move on one soon it'd cost us, was I being money-smart with her not around, was I cooking my own meals or was I eating out every night, and how was it having our loving wonder-dog all to myself? I wrote her back saying having Burnham on my own was nice but because of him I'd been hearing a lot of dead dog stories. I wanted to know: were dead dog stories news to you, or was that normal, to be a dog owner and to be always hearing the dead dog stories of other dog owners? If you didn't know me and you met me at a bar and Burnham was with me, would you tell me a dead dog story, and if so, what dead dog story? I needed to know. I shut my laptop. A second wind of drunkenness blew into me with a do-something sort of heat. All I did was lay down. The bedsheets smelled like beer farts.

I imagined marriage: dim and glassy. I imagined the wedding: sharp and dark. I imagined dating. Dating had no traits.

Burnham's stomach started making hunger-sounds. "Growl" is not the word for these sounds. These sounds snagged up on themselves or tied off into terrible squeaks or rippled wetly or tore open into tight splurching pops, and every one of them could be heard through the comforter I'd pulled over my head. I jumped up in irritation. Burnham sat motionless.

I stomped over him and into the kitchen and slapped his bowl of food. He didn't come until I called three times, his ears flat and his head low. I shook the bowl and told him to eat. He lay with his back to it. "You're hungry," I said, moving the bowl to his face.

His stomach whinnied and squelched.

"Stay," I shouted when he tried to follow me into the kitchen. He cowered. I'd only seen him cower once before. It enraged me. I grabbed a bag of treats and forced him to sit and shake for one. He ate it, crunching slowly. "You like that?" I said, and the fact that I sounded drunk to myself only thickened my anger. I made him sit and shake for a handful of his food, as if it was treats. He took the pellets in his mouth only to let them fall to the floor. They scattered.

I palmed his muzzle and pushed his face into his bowl. I told him to eat. Eat! I pushed harder, jamming him. The food ground under his jaw. He trembled all over like he was sick. I seized him by the scruff, twisted my grip into a fist, and jerked him up and out of the bowl. I thrashed him around. I yelled questions like Now you know to eat? now? now? now? and when I let go to fling him his legs skittered as if he was going to run away. He didn't. He quivered where he was. Looking down at him like that, I saw that I had an erection. It was poking out of my pajamas. It was near-coming.

I sat on the floor and put my dick away. Burnham licked the back of my hand. I was crying, and then I was apologizing, and then I was asleep.

"The day he couldn't shit without falling in it we had him put down," said the steady old man, nodding.

I bought him a drink.

"Fat and blind, with tumors," said the fat young man. "One time she barked blood right into my wife's face."

I bought him a drink.

"Man, that dog could turn on the TV," said the bridesmaid. She was so drunk her eyes blinked independently. "He could change the channels. And he knew how to answer a phone! Smart dog. Spoiled. Slept on the bed. Too big to sleep on the bed."

I bought her a drink.

"He pooped around the Christmas tree. White carpeting. Pooped a circle."

She touched me when she laughed, pressing my shoulder, my elbow, my forearm. She smelled like nail polish. By the time she patted my wrist I saw her wedding band: wide and bright.

"Everybody listened like you listened," she said. "I mean, how about that."

A second bridesmaid yanked her away from me and the bar —I caught the abandoned barstool before it toppled. She didn't come back for the drink I'd bought her that she hadn't touched. I drank it, a leathery scotch.

At home I set the bowl full of food on Burnham's mat. When I called him he began to tremble. He approached with a slow and guilty shuffle. It hurt to see it. I imagined telling my then-fiancée what had happened. It would be hard. We would argue ourselves into a deep silence. And then she'd turn to the work she was always bringing home and stay inside it, and we'd eat and tidy up and sleep, and in a day it would be as if nothing had been said or felt because she'd bury my confession, just as I had buried her confessions, the two of us taking turns, her confessing that she'd at first only looked for a job in the city after graduate school because that's when she met me, but now she liked it, she liked it better than the rural and semi-rural places in Wyoming where she'd grown up, and on account of that she'd be here, with me, forever, and me confessing that I'd only ever lived in different neighborhoods in the same city and sometimes wanted to live in other places where people lived and thought and felt and dreamed differently so that I could through comparison better understand myself. I wanted to miss the city, I confessed.

I am not in anything you just said, she confessed.

These confessions, like the others, went into the ground with the feelings we'd had about hearing them.

Thinking about this made me angry again.

Burnham noticed: he stopped where he was. My anger dropped out of me and I felt awful instead. I gave him a treat, which he ate, then broke up a few more and sprinkled them in his food. "Good boy," I said, and walked to the bedroom. He ignored his bowl and followed me, his stomach whang-gargling. I closed the door before he could get in. He clunked down right outside it.

It was sad, emailed my then-fiancée, that I called these stories "dead dog stories" when everyone else in the world called them "dog stories." Was I okay? Did I need to hang out with my friends in Logan Square? Could I check out the fucking caterer?

I googled, What if your dog won't eat.

I walked him right before mealtimes. I put the bowl in different places in the apartment. I put the food on the floor in front of the bowl. I put fancier food in the bowl. I added olive oil, vegetable oil, raw eggs, cooked eggs, kiszka. Nothing worked. That week he ate only treats. His stomach stopped noise-making and I let him sleep beside the bed. On walks he seemed more excited than usual but more readily exhausted. I brought bags of treats to the Tab and let anyone who wanted to give him one give him one.

At work my friend stopped by my desk. He turned off my monitor. He said I had no choice in the matter, we'd be hitting up the beer-whiskey-pizza special at the Boiler Room, it'd been too long, tough shit. The Boiler Room was five blocks from the Logan Square apartment building where me and my then-fiancée had lived right before we moved to Rogers Park, where my friend, this friend, still lived. We'd shared a wall for three years. Through it, from our respective sides, we'd shouted inane things to each other.

My friend had liked to yell, THIS IS ME TALKING TO MY-SELF.

I said I wanted to hit up the Boiler Room but couldn't, the

dog had been home alone all day. My friend asked when my then-fiancée was coming back. I said another week.

"That's right," he said, remembering. "I don't know how you two do it. Wait," he said, frowning. He farted. He waved it up in my direction.

Later we stood in the elevator lobby, putting on our scarves and gloves. Through the window grainy snow whirled.

He said, "You look run-over."

I didn't say anything. We'd known each other since high school.

He said he'd seen me like this before, and when I asked him when he said the name of an ex-girlfriend, the woman two women before my then-fiancée, a woman I'd had big trouble getting over. The source of the big trouble had been me thinking about her all the time. But that isn't exactly right. It's more that I was feeling things about her all the time, and this frequency of feeling was shoveling up images, images that weren't so much memories as they were dreams, I think, and whatever they were they were heavy and on me and I was under them. I didn't like to think of that woman or that time. I hadn't in years. But when my friend said her name it was as if I'd been feeling things about her all winter, only what was being shoveled up instead of images or memories or dreams about her were images or memories or dreams about dead dogs.

I didn't look at my friend. I didn't want him to know that I was angry at him for showing me this about myself, and more than that, afraid, and more than that, grateful.

He changed the subject while we walked to the Blue Line through the after-work foot traffic, the white collars and the blue collars and the students. He complained about the Bulls, made fun of the mayor, and talked up some new neighborhood brewpub he thought I'd be into. We pushed into the station and through the turnstiles. Our train came. We sat at the back, facing the bobbing door to the car that lurched along behind us. In this other car stood and sat just as many wiped-out men and women, staring and reading and toying with phones. When the train stopped at Jackson I got up to transfer to the Red Line.

My friend whacked my arm. "I'll rustle up the posse. We'll slam it on at your place this Friday."

I said I'd have to spend Friday night working on wedding caterers.

My friend pretended three things: that he believed me, that with enough of his good-natured pressure I'd give in to inviting people over, and that the invited people would readily make the trip to Rogers Park. We bumped fists.

"We hopped in the car and went looking," said the big old woman. "We looked everywhere we could think to look, and then some. It got dark. We went home. I didn't want to go to bed, I wanted to keep looking, so I stayed right by the window and before long I was shouting, 'Mother, it's our dog.' Well, Mother, she was such a sad woman, she said, 'Sweetie, that's the neighbor-dog.' But it wasn't—it was our dog, covered in burrs and mud. How he got there all the way from my aunt's I'll never know."

I bought her a drink.

"Oh no you don't," she said, stopping the spiky-haired bartender. "Don't you go buying old ladies drinks. It seems kind to do but it is not."

"Maybe a month after my mom died," said the amateur stand-up comic, a young woman about my age, "me and my dad were in the pool playing a game where you see who can hold their breath the longest. We were both under, staring each other down, making screwy faces to get each other to laugh, when SPLOOSH!—in jumped the dog. He thought we were drowning. But he was the shittiest swimmer, his hair was clumping up, his hair was sinking him, he was splashing everywhere and making wimpy wet barks, so we had to save him. So sweet and so pathetic at the same time. Is it animal abuse that we were laughing?"

I bought her a drink. I hadn't seen her perform—at the bar my back faced the mini-stage—but she spoke like a performer, with a bouncy lightness that set her just a little outside of what she was saying. She wore a tight t-shirt over a long-sleeved shirt. On her t-shirt a smiling cartoon lemon mounted a squeezer like it was a saddle. The text read something like, WHEN LIFE GIVES ME ME, MAKE MEMONADE.

"I'd like a dog again," she said. "My fiancé's allergic."

She'd been trying to get me to notice her ring: not a diamond, some other colored stone, one that lapped up light discreetly. I told her I didn't really want a dog but I didn't have a choice, this was my fiancée's dog and my fiancée was in Europe for another week.

"How could you not want this dog?" she said to Burnham in a silly dog-voice. "You're so sweet and fluffy! You'd drown too, wouldn't you? Yes! You'd drown!"

Burnham loved her as much as he loved anyone. He pawed at her arms and made goofy frustrated growls when she blew in his ears. I told her how he wouldn't eat his food no matter what I'd tried.

The more I told her about it the more stupid I sounded to myself. At first I thought that how stupid I was sounding had something to do with what I was leaving out, but it was just that I was blushing and trying to hide it by talking. She kissed Burnham between the eyes a bunch of times. The dog she'd grown up with didn't eat sometimes too, she said, and to deal with it she'd started hand-feeding him despite her dad's warning that from then on he'd demand the same treatment at every meal, which he did. She didn't mind. Hand-feeding gave her a funny feeling that she liked. "It's kind of goosebumpy, but on the inside," she said. "It doesn't seem like it should feel good but it does. Vague!

Okay: I guess I mean it's sexual, sexual in a way that has nothing to do with the dog."

I tried to imagine what this meant.

"You've got it," she said, and winked. Then she tapped her nose. And click-clicked her mouth.

I bought her another drink. At her suggestion we swiveled our barstools to watch the other amateur stand-up comics. On the tiny stage they looked sweaty, clumsy, and young. Most of them she knew. She bar-whispered commentary, telling me the famous comics they were ripping off, the drugs they'd done as part of their pre-performance rituals, and one or two wildly inadvisable exploits they'd embarked on late at night after open mikes.

"Look out, here comes Mr. Rape Joke Man," she said.

Mr. Rape Joke Man said, "Two rape jokes walk into a bar. One says, 'Why the long face?' The other says, 'I raped a horse.'"

"I'm out of here," she said.

I got up too.

She scratched Burnham's butt. "You can walk me out!"

The regulars I'd come to know who saw us get up together smiled. The friends who'd come to see her stand-up didn't. Most of them were men. She grabbed her coat from their table and gave out a round of hugs and cheek-kisses. Standing, she was shorter and squarer than she'd seemed on the barstool. She didn't remind me of anyone.

We walked the one block to her car over sharded ice and crunching salt. No wind, just cold. Burnham stayed close to her, pulling hard at his leash. I almost lost my balance more than once. She dance-walked, teasing Burnham.

At her car I asked if she was okay to drive.

"You seem really sober," she said. "How?"

I don't remember what I said but it wasn't witty, and as soon as I'd said it I felt twice as drunk in my face and in my limbs. She jerked open the back door and asked Burnham if he'd like to go for a ride. In he went. "You too," she said, nudging me, "there's no room up front."

Everything in her car smelled like cigarettes except for her. Stacks of crumpled magazines slid around as Burnham paced himself into sitting. In the front passenger seat was a cracked mannequin and a box of wigs.

"I used to be in beauty school," she declared. "I'm a drop-out!"

She drove slowly on residential streets. A few salt-powdered cars circled for parking. I might have asked about her stand-up, or she might have started in on it herself. "A girl's version of 'guy humor.' Instead of dick-and-fart, think vag-and-queef." She told a few jokes that I forgot. I was trying not to think about what anything meant. She was there and saying things and I was sitting there for her to say things to. At my place she parallel-parked in front of a fire hydrant, punched on the flashers, and said she had a question she'd been meaning to ask ever since me and Burnham so nobly walked her out.

"Can I poop out of my anus and into your toilet?"

We took the stairs, Burnham banging on ahead. In the apartment she stepped out of her shoes and made straight for the bathroom. Burnham waited by the door for her, tongue out, tail sweep-wagging. I went to the kitchen, fired on the oven, popped in a frozen pizza, and took two giant glasses of water to the dinner table, where I sat. I couldn't see the bathroom from there but I'd hear her when she got out, which seemed ideal. It seemed so ideal that the contemplation of it gave me satisfaction. I drank my water. I tried to use the feeling of satisfaction to bludgeon the feelings of angry shame, fearful longing, and confusion. I took off my jacket. I drank her water. I refilled her glass in the kitchen and then I went to the bathroom door with it.

I said, "You all right in there?"

I knocked. The door parted some — she wasn't in there. Burnham was missing.

In my terrified rush to check the stairway I dumped her water on myself, dousing my stomach, thighs, and crotch. I crouched to hurry on one boot. When I reached for the other I saw her salt-crusty sneakers still on the mat. That's when I heard sounds in the bedroom.

She sat cross-legged on my bed with Burnham, his bowl of food wedged in her lap. Burnham had never been on a bed before. Up there he looked half his size. She fed him one pellet at a time. She'd taken off her coat.

"Sit down," she said to me.

I sat on the edge of the bed.

"My fiancé is boring," she said. "I love that about him. I love how he wants the same things the same way every day, how he's the same person every hour. He's always himself. He's a happy rock. He can't move on his own. I used to think I wanted to marry an explosion. A series of explosions that would blow me to fucking pieces, that would blow the fucking pieces of me to pieces. Nope. Turns out I don't want that and never did. Here I am: it took me till thirty-five."

"I'm boring," I said. "My fiancée likes me that way. I don't know. I don't get it. I guess I don't like that she likes me that way."

"You try," she said, and she put a pellet in my hand.

I held it out to Burnham. He started trembling.

She put one hand under mine and one hand on Burnham's jaw. She helped him take it from me. He ate it.

"Don't beat your dog," she said.

I didn't say anything.

"Lie down."

I did, tightening up when my soaked jeans chilled me. She took off the one boot I was wearing.

"You pissed yourself," she said, smiling.

I allowed her to believe this.

Burnham sighed.

"Oh," she said.

She was still feeding him, and with her other hand she was touching herself.

She said, "Touch yourself."

I didn't.

Burnham licked the hand she fed him with. She pushed her other hand under her pants and she moaned.

She moaned louder, in a lower voice.

She gripped Burnham's muzzle—he shuffled, afraid—she gripped harder and he whined.

"No," I said, sitting up.

Burnham thumped off the bed and out of the room.

"That's it," I said, "you're done."

She kept at herself, low-moaning with her mouth closed, her back rigid, her hips thrusting.

I watched until it was over.

"I didn't like it here," said my then-fiancée. We were on the couch and not touching, her feet up on her luggage. Burnham, in the other room, had slunk off when we were shouting. We'd agreed to finish out the last month of the lease together. We were exhausted. She looked like she did when I'd get up at two or three, see that I was alone, and find her in the living room sitting on the couch, trying to think herself back to sleep. "I didn't like the city," she said, "I didn't like my dorm and my classes and my professors. I didn't like being away. You know that. But what made it worse was the guy I dated my first semester. We dated for six weeks, which isn't much, but at the time it felt like a lot. He was thoughtful, attentive, playful, handsome. I knew the town in Wyoming he was from. We'd both cut the heads off chickens. He missed his five dogs, I missed my three. After our first week together, he said, 'You ought to break up with me now, because you're going to, later.' I told him not to be so silly. But he started saying stuff like that every day. Then a bunch of times a day. Everywhere we went he made it lonely, which was the opposite of what he'd been doing before that. When I was with him I started to feel more lonely than I did when I was alone. I went from telling him he was silly to telling him he was nervous, mopey, stupid, infuriating, manipulative. But I didn't break up with him. I got mad at him, I sure did, but I apologized, and so did he, and I tried to understand him and his anxieties. I worked at it. I thought he was working at it too. Then he took me on this big date, we went to a classy restaurant on Randolph, the place doesn't exist anymore, I don't even remember what it was called, we ate the kind of food I thought I'd only ever see in movies. After dessert he dumped me. And I'll tell you what: I told myself that that was the last time I'd wait for someone to dump me."

She took her feet off her luggage. It wobbled.

I wasn't sure if she expected me to say something, so I said I didn't think I'd ever dumped anyone.

"He moved to North Dakota and died," she said.

I thought about my other relationships.

She stood up. "Let's take a walk. Let's get a drink."

I told her I shouldn't.

"It's not asking much," she said.

"I'm sorry," I said.

She put on her coat and boots, called the dog, and leashed him on the way out.

At the window I stretched to see them turn the corner. They looked excited.

"I only dumped somebody once," I said to my friend. We were in a booth at the Boiler Room, after work, in front of shots and beer and pizza slices. My friend stopped shaking extra cheese onto his slice to look at me. "We were in college. It wasn't that I didn't like being with her, or didn't love her, it was that I wasn't as wild about her as she was about me. She wanted to be with me all day. It made me feel bad. And I thought that the right thing to do, the respectful thing to do, was to break up."

"Yep," said my friend.

"I dumped her. It was awful for a long time. Afterwards, I thought about it a lot: it seemed it would've just been better to wait it out. To let it go wrong for both of us."

"Nope," he said.

We drank our shots. We were almost drunk.

"What?" he said.

I couldn't remember what I was in the middle of saying, or what I was going to say next.

My friend touched my arm. He said, "You'll think of something else."

Life Story

A man lives with a woman he loves enough to live with, but not enough to marry and not enough for kids. He knows he could love others enough to marry, enough for kids, but he's not the kind of man to find those women when he's with this woman.

Sometimes "love" doesn't fit what he feels. It's too pocket-sized. Or maybe too monumental.

Sometimes "enough" fits. He says to himself, "I don't enough her enough."

"I won't enough her enough."

The woman loves the man enough to live with, enough to marry, enough for kids, but loves him too much to make him into what he won't be. She knows she could find others who love her enough to marry, enough for kids. So what.

Sometimes "love" is too blunt. "Timing" is more textured. "He doesn't timing me yet."

"He won't timing me."

The man is skinny with a robust beard and when he goes for morning walks around the block he keeps his eyes fixed straight ahead. The woman is full-bodied with a bouncy gait and when she's alone she sings opera songs. The two of them aren't traditional in the way their parents are but they're Midwestern enough to want marriage and kids, they can't help it, that's what's in the lives that they imagine.

He stays, and stays, and stays. She knows.

They love living with each other. They get a dog, they play

cards, they cook and bake and slap each other's butts. They share friends, some who marry, some who move away. They both have okay jobs that get better.

They continue loving living with each other except for when they think or talk about marrying and having kids. When they talk about it there is only the restating of statements. They enter their thirties, a banquet hall with no tables or chairs or carpeting.

Years stack up before the both of them. It isn't easy to look away.

The woman thinks, Maybe *I* won't timing him, and when she sings her best songs she feels like biting her wrists, or hugging their dog, or resolving to accept that "love" won't be the word for it when someday soon they'll turn out to have been together forever.

The man thinks, Maybe *she* doesn't enough me enough, and that's because I don't enough her enough, and that's because I don't know why. We don't know why. And somewhere in the middle of his morning walks he closes his eyes, needing to see how many steps he can take until they both scare open on their own.

Company

Brother, yesterday I said to you that there were folks to talk to. That these folks, Mom and me, if talked to, would respond with what we sensed you needed—agreement or advice or humor, say, or silence—and in doing so, offer you what no one can deny needing, the water we pour on our grown-lonely insides: company.

"Company!" our Uncle Nunzo used to shout, the goofball, when we were kids and Mom would take us nearly to the end of the Red Line to see him, when we raced to be the first to punch his buzzer. He'd skip around in cartoony circles, screaming "Help help help, company!" like he'd opened the front door to flames.

"You know that," I said to you, tapping the table, not knowing if you knew it. "You can. You can talk to us."

You said you knew it. I watched you watch your hands scratch the label off your pop bottle. It fluttered in shreds to the floor. I'd guilted you, as you let me do just once a month, to a lonely Mexican joint in the Loop. Mariachi music plugged on around us, going places proudly. If I scooted my chair I smelled bleach and black mold.

You knew it, you said, but you couldn't.

I said, "It's that you *won't*."

You made the face you make when you're trying not to feel what's obvious to everyone.

I made the face I make when I'm trying to stop myself from screaming, You don't understand what's obvious to everyone.

Understand isn't the same as *agree with,* said your face.

My face had nothing to say to that.

When the bill came it came with two candies. I cracked mine in the back of my mouth. You knew I was thinking, If I let you pay, will you feel like you've participated?

You picked up your napkin. I picked up the bill, half of which was my three beers. I hoped for the hundredth time that you'd someday have a drink with us.

"For the holidays," I said, tilting my head this way, that way, "if you come for the holidays, I hope you do, you don't have to talk. Even though you know it's hurt Mom. That you haven't. Talked."

You tore the tiny corners off your napkin.

I gave up: I said, "Thanks for answering my call."

You put down your napkin and said you're welcome but come the new year you'd stop paying for the phone plan you never used.

I didn't know what to make of that—everything inside me sunk.

You folded the napkin and put it in your pocket.

That you intended to no longer have a phone through which we could continue to try to reach you felt even further out than all the other acts of isolation—your acts, my acts, Mom's acts —and made me remember, not for the first time, that for longer than we liked to admit we'd been misunderstanding who we were on purpose.

On the street we shook hands limply, like kids, you wearing your gigantic gloves. Our eyes flicked away just before they met. The meanest wind we'd had all month ripped in from the lake, herding trash, bending everyone who hustled down the block. You walked off wearing the coat I gave you last Christmas—the last Christmas you said you'd ever go to, which was the last thing you said to Mom in person.

"Waitaminute," Mom had said that day, stepping away from the sink, making your exit certain, "scusi, stronzo—per favore, wait wait *wait!*" but you were in that coat and out the door, shutting it so hard the silver bells suicided off. At the window Mom slashed the air with her hands and scourged herself with curses —the first steps of the smashy-dance—as if doing so would get you to look back, to look up as you crossed the courtyard. I crushed her with a hug in case she moved to bust the glass, which she hasn't done since Dad. Together we watched you stiff-walk through old hard snow.

Yesterday I watched you stiff-walk through the Loop's lunch hour foot traffic, between the businessmen and -women, the work-jacketed blue collars, the street-cool students, the poky tourists — tourists even in December, even under all their layers.

"You're a tourist," you said to me years ago, on the first of the lousy Christmases. I'd come home from half a year of living in a different neighborhood, eager to club you with my hipness. That you churned with a bitterness more awful than what I'd expected was in every sentence you didn't say. You were even more alone, and it was and wasn't on me. We moped in the kitchen, not doing dishes, as Mom readied presents in the parlor. I'd been drinking a can of beer because I was old enough. I took manly swigs. I wanted you to want some, to ask for it. You wouldn't. You turned to the sink. I waggled the can in your face, I pressed it to the back of your neck, and that's when you called me a tourist.

Do I need to say what I did next, or why I'm sorry?

I hit you in the head with the can until the can was crushed and foaming.

I'm sorry—I can't stop plunging my head into the past, even though it's hard to breathe in. You know I plunge the most when I've seen you. You know I know you're not actually okay with leaving everything where it is, Mom alone, old wine in old bottles.

"How do you like that," Uncle Nunzo used to say, mock-serious as he sniffed a popped cork. "New wine in a new bottle."

What I'm telling you, brother, is yesterday you walked and I followed, I followed because what you said about your phone plan made it hard for me to get out of my chair. You walked your stiff-walk, which was cocky if not nerdy, your arms looking like they were strapped to your sides, and you whacked shoulders with anyone who didn't give — a many-scarfed grandmother, a jock of a businessman whose bulk nearly knocked you over, who stopped to turn and glare. I waited until you neared the corner, then I hoofed it to catch up, to keep a bead on you. My lungs crackled with lake air. I leaned on a parking meter and burped pukey backwash into my hand.

You puked into Uncle Nunzo's rubber workboots. When we were kids, playing in the mudroom on the plastic rug. Me and Mom thought you'd been faking, acting sick at every Red Line stop to dodge the visit, even though we knew you loved Uncle Nunzo. I didn't want you to turn us around. Watching your miserable face on the train, I'd thought: I can let myself be angry, or not. This knowledge made me feel enormous. After you'd lurched over the toys to yak into both workboots, you wiped your mouth and looked at me that same way — I saw you deciding to be or not be angry. I could have laughed. If I had, you'd have joined me, and before long we'd have slapped the floor and flopped for breath, in cozy hysterics together. Instead I saw my look in your look. I stood up, above you. I grabbed and raised the dripping boots.

The backwash I wiped on my jeans. I managed to keep half a block between us. Your pace was steady except for when you slowed in front of an alley, as if window-shopping. When I got there I slowed too: a grinning two-coated bum sat in a shopping cart, tossing seed to a family of pigeons that muscled dumbly through themselves. "This one, that one, this one," the bum sing-said.

For half an hour you walked an expanding square-like path, a maze you were making from the inside out. That's how I knew you'd lost your job. What I didn't say at the Mexican joint was that I could take the long and beery lunch break because I'd lost my job too.

"A promotion," said Uncle Nunzo, when he got too sick to work, when he was hospitalized. "Pay's different. Different benefits!"

You agreed without saying anything, and he was grateful for it, and I disagreed but said he'd be better soon, and he forgave me for it, and Mom wept in Italian. She always wept in Italian in hospitals.

"Mi rompe i coglioni," she said, and from his bed our laughing Uncle Nunzo took a bow.

When you weren't there he'd say to me, "Always kiss your brother on the head." In his last months he'd demonstrate. "It's easy!"

I want to know: what did he say to you when I wasn't there?

It had to be something, something just as easy.

It had to happen — your squares within squares broke on car-choked Lake Shore Drive, which you crossed. Then you crossed the Lakefront Trail, where bundled cyclists and joggers with sweatered dogs exercised insanely along the lake: a wind-whipped plain of caulk spilled from the sky's bucket. You trudged onto the nearest public pier and all the way to the rail closest to the water, farthest from the city. When you passed an old man he turned and left, as if piers were for one.

I stopped just short of the pier's concrete lip and stomped feeling into my feet on the frozen sand. Behind us, if you'd turned to look, skyscrapers stood, broad and black.

You didn't turn to look. What you did was take out your phone. You held it over the rail and dropped it into the lake.

You took off your glasses, folded them, and dropped them into the lake.

Then your gloves. Your keys. IDs and credit cards and business cards. Your wallet. The napkin.

You unzipped your coat and wriggled out of it and in it went. Your fleece, your button-down, your undershirt—I hadn't seen your torso in ten years—you shook as you undid your belt.

A bearded man in a peacoat jogged past me, to you.

I came up from whatever I was in and into something else, something even worse, and shouted, "It's okay!" to no one.

As you stepped out of your jeans, the bearded man slowed, like you slowed at the alley. He set a hand on your arm. The whole time he was talking.

At first you didn't do anything—you looked like you looked when I slammed the can of beer into the back of your head or dumped the two boots of vomit in your lap or lied and told you, to get you to speak to her, that after the wake Mom had broken both hands while breaking a table, that Mom was out of desperation going to marry Drunken Stanley, that Mom, wanting to make sure she died before you did, had resolved to kill herself with cleaning products.

You sat on the concrete. The bearded man sat next to you, like a dad.

He scooted a bit to unbutton his coat, which he offered you. You shook your head. He put the coat on you anyway. You took it off and gave it back, and said something—a long something, with gestures that went from small to big, from hands to arms—and he listened, his coat on his knees, and when you were done he stood up and pointed back to the city. You said something else, to which he listened, and then you turned to face the lake. He left.

He came towards me, putting on his coat and looking grave.

A young woman had appeared at my side. Pins and buttons

peppered her jacket and a sprout of green hair ran from her knit hat. That she was interested enraged me.

"Think he's okay?" she said.

I looked at her and laughed. I laughed! You're no addict, brother, you're not insane, you haven't been beaten or abused or abandoned. You're okay! You're okay, so what is it, what is it always, and why have we only ever talked around it?

The bearded man came up to her and me with a face that said, I tried, and the young woman hugged him. A kid with a beard, not a bearded man. They were students. Kids.

"I'm going to wait," he said. "Dude might jump."

I said, "Wait for what?"

"The cops," said the girl, "I called them."

"The cops! The cops will tell him to go the fuck away. He'll go the fuck away, they'll go the fuck away, he'll come back and they won't, and if he's going to jump he'll fucking jump. He won't jump."

My voice was high and tight. When I spoke I spat.

The bearded kid came out of hugging his girl in such a way that he stood between her and me. "How do you know?"

Muscles flexed around my heart. I said, "You're crying?"

"I'm—what?"

I peered into his face.

"It's the wind," he said, not backing away. "It's windy."

I grabbed his arm. I was crying.

"Okay," he said. He put an arm around me.

His girl tugged at him but he didn't budge.

A pair of cops passed us, the casual walk they reserve for the homeless.

"He won't jump," I said into the kid's arm.

"Jump," I said when they helped you up, when their hands kept the blanket on your back.

Father's Day

The old man went with his son to a restaurant. The restaurant was in a bowling alley where the old man used to take his son to bowl when his son was a boy. When they sat down, in a booth by the door, the old man said, "This is a terrible place to die."

The son said, "I can't believe we used to bowl here. Remember? Boy, was I lousy."

The old man didn't say anything.

"My wife is pregnant," said the son.

Their food came. It was as expected. The son paid.

Outside it was bright and clear and cool. The son, who had driven, opened the car door for the old man. The old man shuffled in and sat down. He said, "A terrible, terrible place."

The son drove the old man for a long time, for longer than it took to get to the old man's house, the house where the son had grown up. The old man grunted. He tapped the window. The son turned on news radio. They passed a chain of strip malls, a forest preserve, and three ugly rivers. The man on the radio laughed.

When they arrived at the old folks home the son opened the car door for the old man, then the door to the lobby, then the door to the receiving office, and left. A nurse, who was fat, led the old man to his room. It smelled like an airplane smells between flights. Some of the old man's things were already there: sweaters, slippers, pictures of his wife, his son, his son's pregnant wife, and the ticket from the boat that had carried the old man across the ocean from the old country when he'd been an infant.

The old man did not sit down. He said, "This is a terrible place to die."

The fat nurse handed him a cup of water. "All places are terrible places to die."

The old man coughed. That was how he laughed. He drank his water slowly and pointed at the bed. "All places are terrible places."

She shook her head, but in agreement. "All places are places of dying."

"But dying, dying itself is not terrible."

"Believe me," said the nurse, preparing him for his bath, "dying is terrible. Not death. Death can't be terrible."

"Nope, you've got it backwards."

The summer ended. "Tell me," said a different nurse, male, "don't you have a son?"

"You bet I have a son."

The nurse reloaded the old man's IV. "Well, won't you live on through him?"

"I want to read a book."

The nurse helped the old man into a wheelchair and pushed him to the tiny library near the cafeteria. The single bookshelf sagged with thrillers, mysteries, and romances, all donated. The room was empty.

The old man chewed his tongue.

The nurse gave him a cookie and said, "We don't disagree."

"We *do* disagree," said the old man five years later, seated in the cafeteria. He raised his swollen fists. "Dying isn't terrible because dying is knowable, it begins and ends, but death, death is unknowable. Therefore terrible."

This nurse, in her first week of work, laughed. She was young and skinny and she planted her hands on her hips. "Death doesn't end?"

"Right," said the old man, "only dying ends, it ends and that's that. Now how about dessert."

The next day the son returned to the old folks home with the old man's grandson, a quiet little boy. The son offered cookies his wife had baked, but the old man pretended not to smell the cookies and not to know his son and grandson and stared through their heads and chests like they were broken televisions. The son, who was sweating, told a story about this one time when they bowled together, when he was lousy. He pretended to be telling the story to the quiet little grandson but was really telling the story to the old man. He told it three times. The old man wetly cleared his throat.

When they left, the young nurse dressed the old man for bed. "Good of them to come," she said.

"Wasn't terrible. Wasn't good. But could have been either."

"It was terrible," said the nurse, crying.

"Terrible?" he said, and, not wearing any pants or underwear, touched his thigh as she watched. His thigh was soft and gray and stank like Dumpsters in the sun. Then he touched hers, which was dark and firm and smelled like an imaginary fruit.

"I know, I know," she said, and kissed his scalp. She kissed again.

He tried to push her. "Dying! Is! Not! Terrible!"

Ten years later the old man, bedridden, exhaled fiercely and declared: "Dying is terrible."

The young nurse wasn't young anymore. She was pregnant. "What about death."

"Death is a place."

"What kind of place."

The old man waved. "I am a place."

The summer came. The old man was very old.

The grandson returned by himself, a teenager. He looked strange, with strange hair and strange clothes.

The old man met his eyes and said, "You are strange with strange hair and strange clothes but beneath that you are a man, and beneath that you are a place, like me."

The grandson said, "Nice."

The old man grunted. Some of the tubes that were plugged into him rubbed together. "Death is a place."

The grandson gently touched the old man's arm. "We have to move you to a hospice."

"Tell me something that I do not know."

The grandson took his other hand out of his pocket and counted off on fingers: "You don't scare me; I respect you; you may know you are a place but the place itself remains unknown; the known is more terrible than the unknown; my dad won't tell us he has cancer and always wants to take us bowling but when we go he can't even throw the ball, he just starts crying and runs outside and waits in the car and when we knock on the window he gets out and pretends like he just showed up; my mom is awesome, super-awesome, she's teaching me how to bake; my girlfriend's pregnant; I'm not so sure I'm straight; today is Father's Day; happy Father's Day."

The old man touched his grandson's face. He began to die. "That's good," he said to his grandson. "Don't go."

Acknowledgments

A writer writes a book with lots of help. This book wouldn't be here if it weren't for many incredible people, people I am deeply fortunate and grateful to know. Eleanor Jackson, thank you for your belief, your patience, and your savvy. Jenna Johnson and Pilar Garcia-Brown, thank you for your generous vision, for your brilliant challenges, and for enriching everything you touch. Thank you to David Hough for insightful and rigorous copyediting. Thank you to the literary magazine editors and contest judges who published some of this collection's pieces in earlier forms: Zach Bean, David Ryan, Chris Boucher, Vaughan Simons, David H. Lynn, Carmen Giménez Smith, Evan Lavender-Smith, Jacob White, Christina Harrington, Analicia Sotelo, Aimee Bender, Katie Berta, Roxane Gay, Jensen Beach, Jeremy "Holy Good Goddamn!" Schraffenberger, Bridget G. Dooley, Laurie Ann Cedilnik, Joey Pizzolato, Allegra Hyde, Dana Diehl, and T. Kira Madden, with special thanks to David McLendon, for seeing this book before I did, and to Matt Bell, for the gift of your friendship. Robert Boswell, Kevin McIlvoy, and Antonya Nelson, the high desert trinity of fiction mentors: I haven't stopped saying thank you, and won't. CJ Hribal, thank you for telling me what an MFA is and for helping me get to one. Larry Watson, thank you for talking to me like I was a writer and for years of invaluable advice. Thank you to Amelia Zurcher and Rebecca Nowacek. Glen Brown and Kate Singletary: thank you for putting light into the lives of so many young writers. Dr. Van Lear: it all fits together. Do you know how often I talk about you? Bless you. Claire Vaye Watkins and Derek Palacio, thank you for saying, "Send the book out," for that email, and for WT-ery. Nathan Graham and Michelle Mariano, thank you for the mountain and for potlucks, for so much time in so many cities: for the nonstop friendsgiving. Thank you to Stephen Lloyd Webber and Jade Webber for the Yard and Oakhaven, for golden b's and green shooting stars. Dave Bachmann, thank you for the tradition of Chicago bar book-talks. Austin Tremblay, thank you for CCL. Thank you to the New Mexico State University crew, especially Parker Staley, Heather Hermann, Lindsay Armstrong, Jeff Vance, Melanie Viramontes, Nicky Pesseroff, Dana Kroos, Lillie Robertson, Jason Ronstadt, Michaela Spampinato, Cara Olexa, Carrie Grinstead, Ryan Orr, Skye Anicca, Stefan McKinstray, Jill Stukenberg, Travis Brown, Justin Chrestman, Josette Arvizu, Jeff Frawley, David MacLean, Rus Bradburd, Connie Voisine, Sheila Black, and Sarah Hagelin. Thank you to the University of Houston crew, especially J. Kastely, Alex Parsons, Chitra Divakaruni, ZZ Packer, Hosam Aboul-Ela, David Mazella, Jameelah Lang, Whit Bones, Talia Mailman, The Real Katie Condon, Sir Conor Bracken, JP Gritton, Thomas "Boot Brother" Calder, Julia Brown, Elizabeth Winston, Nancy Pearson, Selena Anderson, Tyson Morgan, Chris Hutchinson, Megan Martin, David Tomás Martinez, Claire Anderson, Sara Rolater, Greg Oaks, Bryan Owens, and Zach Martin. Ed Porter and Jacqui Sutton, as promised: thank you for the chair. Thank you to Heather Sartin and Peter Graham, Dan Chelotti, Odin-eyed birch-wizard, amico: there's a myth for this. Thank you to the Susquehanna University crew, especially Gary Fincke, Glen Retief, Peterson Toscano, Tom Bailey, Susan Bowers, Randy Robertson, and Nick Ripatrazone. Karla Kelsey: bloodfeather swanfang forever. Thank you to Catherine Zobal Dent and Silas Dent Zobal for your wisdom and love and laughter. Moustaches to Elizabeth Deanna Morris and Kenny Lakes, Will Hoffacker and Dana Diehl, Melissa Goodrich, David Joseph, Kim Stoll, Mike Coakley, and Sarah Gzemski. Thank you to my extraordinary Bucknell University colleagues in the English Department, especially Paula Closson Buck, Robert Rosenberg, Shara McCallum, GC Waldrep, Chris Camuto, Denise Lewis, Andy Ciotola, Katie Hays, John Rickard, Ghislaine McDayter, Carmen Gillespie, and Harry Bakst. Thank you to the good people of the Bucknell University Theatre and Dance Department. Thank you, thank you, thank you to my students. Thank you to current and former Lewisburgers: Erica Delsandro, Pete Groff and Maria Balcells, Logan and Elise Connors, Nathalie Dupont, Amanda Wooden and John Enyeart, Bob and Iris Gainer, Deirdre O'Connor, Peg Cronin, Porochista Khakpour, Lazslo Strauss, Darren Hick, Chipper Dean, John Bourke, Ben Jones, Beth "Practical Visionary" Duckles, and Alex "Blood Moon Brother" Lumans. Thank you to James Tadd Adcox, Scott Onak, Matt Rowan, A.D. Jameson, Ted Gerstle, and Jacob Singer. Jeffrey Jeffecito Glodek, Professoressa Shawna Hennessey, David Slicer Miller, Vera Miller, the Wild Doty, Nikkity Crickets, Kelsey Belsey, Andrew Roddewig, Bart Davis, Meagan Kadlec, George Perry, Mary and William Martin, Sarah and Chad, Farnypoo, the McGrabbits, Crusher, Real World Reid and Debra, Lucy Kim, Double J Turowski, David Peak, Will Petty—slammit on, chombattas. Thank you to Bill from Marlins, for the questions. Thank you to the Martincichs and the Horvaths and the Stefanichs and the Kaskys and the Smiths, with special thanks to mia suocera Debbie. Thank you to the Gackis and the Kostals and the Scapellatos and the Cocos, with special thanks to Aunt Judy and Uncle Ken, Aunt Paula, Tom and Megan, Forrest and Tamara, Louie and Anthony, and the mighty Bronek. Thank you, Judy Murphy. Thank you, Mom and Dad, for showing everyone who knows you how to love people and life and language, and for much more than can fit here. Thank you to Vittorio and Matthew for being writers before me, for showing me the wonder of it. Thank you to Mario for reading everything I've ever written, more than once, and for being honest always. Thank you to Jen for wisdom and warmth and always asking. Thank you to Arik and Garrett: you're natural twenties. And thank you to Dustyn, best friend, first reader — big love, no lonesome — bopadoo.